Praise for *This Journal Belongs to Ratchet*

"A book that is full of surprises...Triumphant enough to make readers cheer; touching enough to make them cry."

—*Kirkus* Starred Review

"Cavanaugh uses bold, often humorous first-person narration to capture the essence of an unconventional heroine struggling to figure out who she is supposed to be. Ratchet's journal...offers an enticing blend of strong social views, family secrets, and deeply felt emotions."

—*Publishers Weekly*

"Perfect for anyone who feels she doesn't belong."

—*Discovery Girls*

"Ratchet is a thoroughly relatable character whose wish for normalcy will strike a chord with readers."

—*Booklist*

"Girls who do not fit in or who move often will find a piece of themselves in Ratchet's story."

—*Library Media Connection*

"Bottom line: I cannot imagine a middle grade classroom or library where this book wouldn't be popular."

—Colby Sharp, *sharpread*

"Ratchet is a memorable heroine; the vivid portrayal of what it's like to have no money for nice clothes and other things Americans take for granted will give readers something to think about."

—*The Buffalo News*

"One of the freshest new voices I've heard in a while...A book for young readers to enjoy, discuss, then read all over again, this debut novel is a winner."

—Augusta Scattergood, award-winning author of *Glory Be*

Also by Nancy J. Cavanaugh

This Journal Belongs to Ratchet

ALWAYS, ABIGAIL

NANCY J. CAVANAUGH

sourcebooks
jabberwocky

Published by Sourcebooks Jabberwocky, an imprint of Sourcebooks, Inc.
P.O. Box 4410, Naperville, Illinois 60567-4410
(630) 961-3900
Fax: (630) 961-2168
www.jabberwockykids.com

Library of Congress Cataloging-in-Publication data is on file with the publisher.

Source of Production: Worzalla, Stevens Point, WI, USA
Date of Production: June 2014
Run Number: 5001873

Printed and bound in the United States of America.
WOZ 10 9 8 7 6 5 4 3 2 1

A cousin wave to Marissa, Adam, Kiera,
Lexie, Kelsie, Isaac, and Austin

THE COOLEST THING ABOUT SIXTH GRADE

The pom-pom squad!!!!!

THREE REASONS MAKING POM-POMS IS MORE IMPORTANT THAN ANYTHING ELSE

1. Alli and Cami, my two best friends, and I saw the Crestdale Heights pom-pom girls for the first time when we were in third grade. It was love at first sight! The sequined outfits, the hats, the pom-poms, and the music. We looked at each other after the first routine and knew why we'd all been born: to be POM-POM GIRLS.

Since then, we've made up exactly seventeen different routines. We've talked our moms into buying us five different matching outfits. And we've downloaded ninety-eight songs we can use for pom-pom routines.

All three of our families, especially our brothers (we each have one), wish we'd never seen those pom-pom girls. But the three of us know that was the day we found our DESTINY.

2. <u>Everyone</u> who's <u>anyone</u> is a pom-pom girl.

At Crestdale Heights Middle School, pom-pom girls are practically celebrities.

(Okay, Crestdale Heights isn't <u>really</u> a middle school; it's <u>really</u> Crestdale Heights K through 8. But the little K through 5 kids are NOT allowed in the middle school hallway, so it's sort of like a real middle school.)

On game days, pom-pom girls get to wear their uniforms to school. It's like Oscar night on the red carpet, and the pom-pom girls are wearing the best designer in town.

3. BOYS.

Boys notice pom-pom girls. (Even seventh- and eighth-grade boys.) And once they notice them, they talk to them, they hang out with them, and eventually...(Okay, I'm not really sure what comes next, but who cares?!)

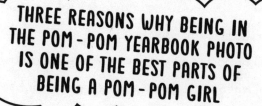

ONE MORE REASON MAKING POMS IS MORE IMPORTANT THAN ANYTHING ELSE

The pom squad always gets their photo in the yearbook.

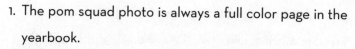

THREE REASONS WHY BEING IN THE POM-POM YEARBOOK PHOTO IS ONE OF THE BEST PARTS OF BEING A POM-POM GIRL

1. The pom squad photo is always a full color page in the yearbook.

2. The pom squad photo hangs in the trophy case hallway for everyone to see, and the pom squad photos go all the way back to the 1980s, which means our photo would be there for a REALLY long time.

3. At the end of the season, Ms. Jenson, the pom coach, always gives each girl on the squad a shoulder bag with

3

the pom squad photo printed on it. I can't wait to walk around school every day with that bag hanging over my shoulder.

FIVE REASONS WHY I WRITE LISTS

1. I have the BEST handwriting.

   (I'm not bragging here. It's the truth. Up until fourth grade, when we stopped getting a grade for handwriting, I always got A's in penmanship. In fact, it was always my only A.)

2. I love buying cute notebooks and filling them up.

3. Lists are much cooler than, "Dear Diary, Blah, blah, blah..."

   (I mean really, I already did that whole "Dear Diary" thing way back in third grade, and I'm so over it.)

4. People who write lists are more likely to succeed.

   (I'm pretty sure that's a proven fact. I just can't remember who proved it.)

5. I LOVE writing lists!

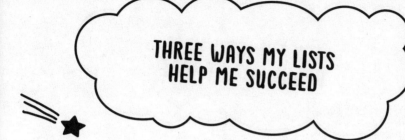

THREE WAYS MY LISTS HELP ME SUCCEED

1. I'm a superorganized person, and my lists help me stay organized.

2. When your grades are just so-so like mine, turning in your work on time helps. My lists help me never miss an assignment. (My neatness helps too. Neat, on-time assignments usually get pretty good grades even when all the answers aren't right.)

3. My lists calm me down. When I'm overwhelmed and anxious and feel like I can't get everything done, I write a list. Some of my teachers have told my parents that if I spent as much time on my schoolwork as I do on my lists, I'd be a much better student. What they don't understand is that without my lists, I wouldn't be able to get anything done.

TEN THINGS I HATE ABOUT SIXTH GRADE

1. Alli and Cami (aka AlliCam) are NOT in my homeroom.

2. Ditto

3. Ditto

4. Ditto

5. Ditto

6. Ditto

7. Ditto

8. Ditto

9. Ditto

10. Ditto

ONE REALLY SUPERSWEET THING ALLICAM DID FOR ME

Gave me an AlliCam Withdrawal Survival Kit.

FOUR THINGS INSIDE THE ALLICAM WITHDRAWAL SURVIVAL KIT

1. A photo to hang in my locker of the three of us at camp last summer.

2. A blue, braided friendship bracelet.

   (They each have one exactly the same.)

3. A luggage tag for my backpack that says, "SPF— SISTERS, POMS, FRIENDS."

4. A small spiral notebook perfect for writing notes to them.

   (The front cover of the notebook has three kittens on it that they labeled Abigail, Alli, and Cami. Then they drew little purple pom-poms in each one of the kittens' paws and wrote at the top, "POMS FOREVER.")

THREE THINGS I'M THANKFUL FOR

1. The orthodontist said I don't have to get my braces until January. So I don't have to start middle school with a mouth full of metal. Yay! Most importantly, I won't have to be happy hardware face at pom-pom tryouts.

2. My hair is finally normal after the perm disaster.

   Alli and Cami both have wavy hair, and I love, love, love it! So I begged my mom for a perm. She tried to talk me out of it, but since <u>she's</u> the reason I have such straight, boring, lifeless hair (hers is exactly the same way), she felt bad for me and gave in.

   Man, I wished I could've pressed the rewind button that day. I walked out of the salon looking like a big-headed poodle. Ugh! I told the lady <u>waves</u> not <u>curls</u>. But adults just don't get it sometimes. At least it was the beginning of the summer, and I didn't have to go to school. Mom took me back to the salon the next day for a haircut, and I got most of it cut off. My hair was <u>super</u>short. I hated it! But it was better than being POODLE GIRL all summer. My hair was finally back to normal length the week before school started. Whew!

3. AlliCam and I have the coolest clothes for school this year. Shopping was, like, a full-time job for us this summer.

THE LIST I MADE FOR OUR SUMMER SHOPPING SCHEDULE

1. Sundays: collect sale ads from the newspaper.
2. Mondays: circle everything we like.
3. Tuesdays: get my mom to drop us at the mall.
4. Wednesdays: get Cami's mom to drop us at the outlet center.
5. Thursdays: get Alli's mom to drop us at the thrift shop.
6. Fridays and Saturdays: try on everything we bought and decide if we really like it.

We planned to shop like this all summer, but we ran out of birthday and babysitting money after two weeks. So we spent the rest of the summer making up more pom-pom routines and practicing them.

THREE REASONS WE RAN OUT OF BIRTHDAY AND BABYSITTING MONEY SO QUICKLY

1. We all have winter birthdays. AlliCam's birthdays are in January. Mine is February, so none of us had much birthday money left by summertime.

2. AlliCam both got sick of their babysitting jobs. The families they babysat for had only boys, and they were monsters, so they both stopped babysitting.

3. I liked the kids I babysat for, but I didn't like babysitting on Friday and Saturday nights when AlliCam were together doing fun things without me like makeovers, manicures, and workout videos. I hated missing out on all that, so I kept saying I was busy when the moms asked me to babysit, and eventually they stopped asking me. (My mom was not too thrilled once she realized what had happened, but AlliCam were my best friends. What was I supposed to do?)

A FEW THINGS I'M NOT SO THANKFUL FOR

1. Even with the poodle-perm incident behind me, my hair is nothing to brag about. Its color: dirty dishwater. (Doesn't that sound attractive?) Its style: nonexistent because it's as limp as a dirty dishrag. (Doesn't that sound fashionable?) Its condition: oily and dull thanks to the hormones of puberty—that's what Mom says. (Doesn't that sound disgusting?)

2. So I do the best I can with what I have, and mostly I wear my dirty, dishrag hair in a ponytail. It's better than the poodle look, but not by much. The worst part is that AlliCam's hair is amazing—not only is it wavy, but it's perfectly conditioned, shiny, shampoo-commercial hair. Alli's is blond, and Cami's is black. Perfect hair colors.

3. The coolest clothes don't hide the fact that I don't have the coolest body. I don't know what it is, but I can be wearing the same exact outfit as AlliCam (even the same size), and somehow it always looks better on them.

4. And then there's the braces thing. I'm glad I'm not getting them on for a while, but it'd be better if I didn't have to get them at all. Why couldn't I have been born with straight teeth like AlliCam? I mean, I've got the bad hair, the so-so body. Would it have been too much to ask to just have good teeth?

SOMETHING REALLY FUN ALLICAM AND I DID OVER THE WEEKEND

Alli's dad let us use his camera, and we did a pom-pom girl photo shoot. We decorated a huge poster with Crestdale Heights Middle School written on it for the background. I did the lettering on the sign, so of course it looked amazing! Then we put on one of our favorite outfits that we bought last summer, and we posed with our pom-poms. We even turned a fan on to blow our hair around, so we'd look like real models.

We took about a <u>million</u> pictures until we each got one that we LOVED. (Well, I got one that I "liked." None of mine were quite as good as AlliCam's.) Then we printed the photos on Alli's brother's computer and used her mom's mini-laminator to make ID cards to carry on our gym bags.

They turned out soooo CUTE!

SOMETHING THAT WAS SUPPOSED TO BE THE BEST THING ABOUT SIXTH GRADE IS TURNING OUT TO BE THE WORST THING

In sixth grade, instead of being stuck with the <u>same</u> boring teacher, talking in the <u>same</u> boring way, ALL day long, each homeroom gets to switch to a different teacher for each subject. But without Alli and Cami in my homeroom, it means I get <u>different</u> boring teachers, but no AlliCam ALL day long—just the SAME boring, geeky classmates ALL day, EVERY day, ALL YEAR LONG.

ANOTHER WORST THING ABOUT SIXTH GRADE

Hi Sweetie! I love you! Love, Mom xo

Lunch.

My homeroom doesn't have lunch at the same time as AlliCam's, so I'm stuck eating lunch with Jeannie and Marcy.

It's not that they're so bad—it's just that, well, they're kind of prissy and a little babyish. Like their moms still write little "I love you" notes and put them in their lunches. I'd die if my mom did that!

(My mom still writes me messages in the foggy bathroom mirror when I'm in the shower. "I ♥ U! ☺" I do still like that, but nobody knows about *that*.)

Then there's Jeannie's and Marcy's clothes. Well, let's just say, I saw a second-grader on the bus wearing the same outfit Marcy had on the other day. If that happened to me, I would've faked sick so I could go home. Not Marcy—she kept calling the kid her little twin.

I don't want anyone thinking the three of us are really good friends. That wouldn't do much for my image.

So I sit close enough to them so that it doesn't look like I'm sitting alone, but not too close.

TEN MORE THINGS I HATE ABOUT HOMEROOM

1. Miss Hendrick (aka Hendrick-the-Horrible-Hundred-Year-Old Hawk) is my homeroom teacher.
2. Ditto
3. Ditto
4. Ditto
5. Ditto
6. Ditto
7. Ditto
8. Ditto
9. Ditto
10. Ditto

THREE REASONS SHE'S CALLED "HENDRICK-THE-HORRIBLE-HUNDRED-YEAR-OLD HAWK"

1. She's horrible. You just have to know her; no explanation needed.

2. She's got to be at <u>least</u> one hundred years old by now. (My mom had her when <u>she</u> was in sixth grade.)

3. She sees EVERYTHING that goes on—that's why she's called the Hawk. She doesn't just have eyes in the back of her head. She's got eyes in the hallway, in the bathroom (boys <u>and</u> girls), and on the playground. No one knows how she does it.

THREE THINGS MOM TOLD ME ABOUT OLD HAWK

1. She's the strictest teacher in the whole school.
2. She's the toughest teacher in the whole school.
3. Someday you'll appreciate her for that.

ONE QUESTION I ASKED MOM

Are you kidding me?

ONE THING MOM SAID

You'll see.

THE REASON I HATE LANGUAGE ARTS

Old Hawk is my homeroom teacher AND my language arts teacher.

THREE REASONS I HATE HAVING LANGUAGE ARTS WITH OLD HAWK
(THERE'RE 181 DAYS LEFT OF SCHOOL. I'M SURE THERE'LL BE MORE REASONS.)

1. She's so last century with her old lady glasses hanging on a chain around her neck. And her clothes—you should see them. Plaid, polyester skirts, frilly blouses, and neck scarves. She must be in the witness protection program using our school as a hideout from the fashion police. She's a makeover waiting to happen. And you should

see her hair. It looks like it's older than she is. Actually, it looks like an old man's beard piled on top of her head.

I'm surprised she doesn't ride to school in a covered wagon.

2. She doesn't like computers. Doesn't think we should use them for our writing assignments. She says, "Young people today have lost the art of language the way it was intended to be written and spoken."

I think <u>she's</u> the one who's losing it because no one even knows what she's talking about half the time.

The first day of school she passed out penmanship paper. You know, the kind kindergarten teachers use. Then she hung up one of those alphabet strips across the top of the chalkboard. She actually made us practice printing our full names in perfect penmanship.

The other kids were going nuts—complaining, whining, and whispering to each other, "Doesn't she know this is sixth grade?" "She's crazier than everyone says she is."

I joined the crowd by doing a few eye rolls and a couple huge sighs, but secretly, I was loving it as I watched my perfect letters fill up the big wide spaces between the lines. My paper looked awesome! Even better than Old Hawk's example on the board.

I wondered if the principal knew she was doing stuff like this. Maybe I should report her. I could write an anonymous letter:

Dear Mr. Buckley,

Do you know that one of your sixth-grade teachers is a kindergarten teacher disguised as a middle school teacher? You must act now. She's teaching penmanship instead of punctuation. Save the sixth-graders in 6H from this cruel and unusual punishment. Remove her from her classroom before it's too late.

Yours truly,
Anonymous

3. The biggest reason I hate having Old Hawk for language arts—THE FRIENDLY LETTER assignment!

    She gave a twenty-minute speech about how she has an "ax to grind" with the "youth of America." (She's famous for her speeches. Even my mom talks about them.) This one was about how she is "sick as a horse" to see young people using letters and numbers for words when they type e-mails and text messages.

22

She wrote **"BF4EVAH"** on the board. "<u>This</u> is not writing, my friends."

(She always calls us "her friends" when she's making one of her speeches.)

Her solution to this horrific writing crime against humanity: THE FRIENDLY LETTER ASSIGNMENT.

"As a way to practice writing the English language as it was intended, each of you will be assigned a partner."

(The key word here: <u>assigned</u>.)

"You will write letters to your partner once a week. You will WRITE these letters. Not type them. Not text message them. Not telepathically transmit them. You will use your best handwriting. You will spell words correctly. You will use proper grammar <u>and</u> punctuation. Am I clear?"

No one said anything, but I knew everyone wished they could write Old Hawk a friendly letter asking...

AN OMINOUS (ONE OF OLD HAWK'S FIRST VOCAB WORDS) WARNING OLD HAWK GAVE ABOUT OUR FRIENDLY LETTER ASSIGNMENT

"My friends, do you realize that the United States government protects our mail? It is actually a federal offense for anyone to tamper with the U.S. mail. Which means it is an offense punishable by the law; and in our classroom, our friendly letters will be treated with the same utmost respect. No one, except the recipient, may read the friendly letters you write. No one, except you, may read the friendly letters you receive, and even I, the postmaster general of this classroom, am not above this law. So you should rest assured that I will not be reading your letters.

"To summarize," Old Hawk said while writing on the board, "the friendly letters written in this classroom are private property between you and your friendly letter partner," and she underlined *private property* three times.

"That said, I am certain that no one, not a single one

24

of you, my friends, will abuse this privilege of privacy and/or misuse it to write anything that would not be mature and respectful in nature."

NUMBER ONE REASON I HATE MY LIFE THIS YEAR

Gabby Marco is my friendly letter partner. She's the biggest LOSER in the WHOLE school. Something like this could ruin a person's life.

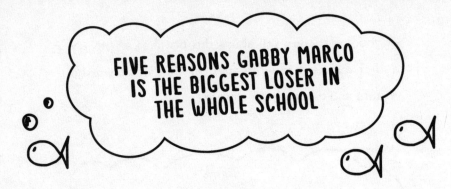

FIVE REASONS GABBY MARCO
IS THE BIGGEST LOSER IN
THE WHOLE SCHOOL

1. The first time anyone even noticed Gabby was fourth grade. That's when Brent Undervale raised his hand when we were thinking up rhyming words for our poetry unit. Mrs. Nagle called on him, and nobody could believe it, but he actually said, "<u>Flabby</u> and <u>Gabby</u>." (He got sent to Mr. Buckley's office, and his mom had to come and get him.)

   Gabby <u>is</u> a little on the chubby side, but she's not really <u>fat</u>. The thing is, at Crestdale Heights, once someone says something like that about you, whether it's true or not, it sticks to you and follows you around like toilet paper on your shoe.

2. The second reason isn't even Gabby's fault, really. It's because of what happened last year on the bus with Jackson Dawber.

   Everyone knew that Gabby had lived with her aunt until the beginning of fifth grade. That's when she moved in with her older brother. Everyone thought that was a little strange since her brother was only in high school. No one knew why she didn't live with her parents, and no one cared enough to find out.

Anyway, after Christmas break, our bus route changed, and Gabby's new stop was right in front of her house. When everyone saw where Gabby lived, they stared out the window at her house like it was a burning building. The house was really more like a dented-up trailer attached to a "dilapidated" (to use one of Old Hawk's vocab words) barn that was falling down. It looked like if you slammed the front door too hard, the whole thing would collapse.

That's when Jackson (whose dream is to become a stand-up comic) started yakking like he always does.

Using the highlighter he carries around all the time as a microphone, he yelled out, "If that house were a boat, it would sink. If it were a plane, it would fall out of the sky. If it were a car, there's no way it would run..."

Jackson's jokes are so lame-o. Everyone knows he'll never make it as a comedian. Even so, kids laugh.

Gabby was off the bus when Jackson started blathering, but I'm pretty sure she heard what Jackson said. She had to have at least heard all the laughing.

Once the bus was back on its way, I remember wondering what Gabby's house looked like on the inside; and for the first time, I wondered what had happened to her parents.

3. The biggest reason Gabby Marco is the number one outcast at Crestdale Heights: she laughs sometimes for no reason at all. Usually it's when she has her head buried in one of the old paperback books she always carries around, but that's not the only time she laughs like that. It's <u>really</u> weird. The classroom can be perfectly quiet, and she'll start giggling. And then start laughing.

Some kids say she's crazy or possessed or something. Why else would someone laugh for no reason at all?

4. and 5. I thought there were more reasons no one liked her, but I guess that's it.

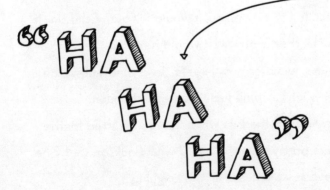

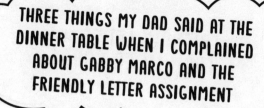

THREE THINGS MY DAD SAID AT THE DINNER TABLE WHEN I COMPLAINED ABOUT GABBY MARCO AND THE FRIENDLY LETTER ASSIGNMENT

1. "Miss Hendrick must have a method to her madness."

2. "Once you get to know Gabby, you might feel differently about her."

3. "Maybe it's *destiny*, Abs."

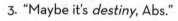

THREE THINGS I TOLD MY DAD

1. "I think madness is a good way to describe Old Hawk."

2. "The problem is I don't <u>want</u> to get to know Gabby."

3. "Old Hawk's friendly letters and Gabby Marco CANNOT be my *destiny*!"

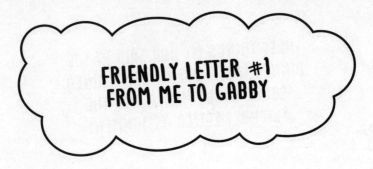

FRIENDLY LETTER #1
FROM ME TO GABBY

Dear Ms. Gabriella Marco,

I am your letter partner.

The most important thing in my life is pom-poms. Alli and Cami from 6B are my best friends, and we all can't wait until we're officially part of the squad.

Here are a few other things about me. I am in sixth grade like you. I have one older brother like you. My favorite food is pizza. My favorite dessert is chocolate cake. My favorite book is *Ella Enchanted*. I hate mushrooms, pumpkin pie, and that stupid book *Hatchet* we read last year for Mr. Kirby.

Sincerely,
Abigail Walters

THINGS TO DO

1. Write first friendly letter <u>to</u> Gabby.
2. Dread getting my first friendly letter <u>from</u> Gabby. ✔
3. Begin counting down the 179 days until this insanely stupid friendly letter assignment is over. ✔
4. Pray Gabby's weirdness doesn't rub off on me. ✔
5. Celebrate after writing my very last friendly letter to Gabby.

THE NOTE I LEFT IN ALLICAM'S LOCKER
(ALLI AND CAMI ARE NOT ONLY IN THE SAME HOMEROOM, BUT THEY'RE LOCKER PARTNERS TOO. SOOOO LUCKY!)

Dear AlliCam,

Old Hawk is a real prob. We have to write "friendly letters" to ASSIGNED partners. Guess who I got? GABBY MARCO. Can you believe it?

    You guys are so lucky to be in 6B TOGETHER!!!!

SPF—Sisters, Poms, Friends,

Abigail

THE NOTE I FOUND IN MY
LOCKER AFTER LUNCH

Dear Abigail,

We miss you!!!! Wish you were here. Blah, blah, blah.
Gabby Marco?! EEEEK! We're sorry!

SPF,
AlliCam

THREE REASONS ALLI, CAMI, AND I ARE BEST FRIENDS

1. We sat at the same table the first day of kindergarten, and as they say, the rest is history. All that coloring, finger painting, and playing dress-up bonded us for life.

2. All three of us LOVE the same thing: talking. When Cami's dad drove us to camp last summer, it took five hours to get there. We NEVER ran out of things to talk about. Cami's dad thought we should enter the *Guinness World Records* book for the longest conversation.

3. None of us have sisters, so in fifth grade, we did a Native American sister ritual. (There wasn't really anything Native American about it, but our teacher had just finished reading *The Indian in the Cupboard*, so we were sort of in a Native American phase.)

    We did the ritual in Alli's backyard one night when we slept over at her house. We put some paint stirrers in the barbecue grill and lit them on fire. Then we held hands and walked in a circle around the grill chanting,

"Sister fire from long ago,
Make us sisters from head to toe.
Flames and smoke keep us strong.
Forever we'll sing our sister song."

(Cami made up the chant. She's really good at stuff like that. She won first prize in the school poetry contest last year.)

Then we danced around and sang,

"We are family.
I got all my sisters with me..."

(It wasn't a Native American song. We'd heard it on the oldies station, but it was perfect for our ritual.)

After a few choruses of "We Are Family," Alli's dad came outside, and we got in big trouble for being too loud, but when he saw the fire, we got in even bigger trouble for that. He told us if it wasn't so late, he'd send Cami and me home.

We thought getting into trouble for doing the ritual just made our sisterhood bond even stronger. And once Alli's dad went back upstairs, we couldn't stop laughing about how hysterical he looked standing on the back porch in his boxers with his hair all messed up and yelling, "Are you girls out of your minds? It's one o'clock in the morning! Get your butts inside right now or you're going to be singing 'Sorry.'"

When we got back inside, Alli kept standing on the fireplace hearth and imitating her dad. "You girls are gonna be singing 'Sorry.'"

Cami and I kept raising our hands like we were in school and saying, "Excuse me, Mr. Martin, but we don't know that song."

Then the three of us collapsed onto the floor in a heap of laughter. Every time we did it, it got funnier.

It just proved the three of us were meant to be best friends <u>and</u> sisters.

THREE REASONS I HATE BEING IN A DIFFERENT HOMEROOM FROM ALLICAM

1. Inside jokes. When we go to each other's houses after school, Cami and Alli are always talking about things that happened in school. I never know what they're talking about. Yesterday, they looked at each other and put their thumbs under their chins, waved, and then burst out laughing. I laughed too even though I didn't know why it was so funny. When I did it later, they looked at each other and rolled their eyes. Is this how the whole year's going to be?

2. Extra pom practice. Every day AlliCam and I practice poms together after school. Alli and Cami also practice at school after lunch. But since I don't have the same lunch period as they do, they're getting a lot of extra practice without me. What if I'm not practicing enough?

3. Mr. Blue Eyes. While I'm stuck with Old Hawk, AlliCam's class has a brand-new teacher. You should see him! He's gorgeous! He looks like a surfer from California with all

that bleached blond hair and those bulging biceps. That's why everyone calls him Mr. Blue Eyes. (Well, not the boys.) I don't see how <u>anyone</u> could learn <u>anything</u> from someone who looks sooooo good. I should really write another anonymous letter to the principal.

Dear Mr. Buckley,

Are you aware that there's a swimsuit model here at Crestdale Heights disguised as a first-year teacher? Sixth-grade girls CANNOT learn from someone like this. Think about how impossible it is to underline nouns and circle verbs in a sentence when you're drooling over the teacher. This man should be removed from the premises immediately.

Maybe Mr. Whitmar could come out of retirement until you find a replacement. (Hopefully one who is not so cute!)

Yours truly,
Anonymous

THINGS TO DO

1. Work on making up some inside jokes about things that happen on the bus with AlliCam.

2. Practice poms an extra hour at home to make up for AlliCam's lunch practice.

3. Pray that Old Hawk gets a student teacher second quarter—hopefully a supercute "guy" student teacher who will persuade Old Hawk to end the friendly letter assignment once and for all. (Even though I didn't see this ever happening, I prayed for it anyway.)

ONE BIG REASON TO PANIC ABOUT POM-POM TRYOUTS

There's a new sixth-grader who just transferred to Crestdale Heights. She's not just any new student; she's Alicia Brenton. <u>The</u> Alicia Brenton. Her older sister is practically the pom-pom poster girl from one of our rival schools. But thanks to rezoning, Alicia's now in our district. This could mean trouble for me. BIG trouble.

There are six spots on the sixth-grade squad. Here's the breakdown: Alicia Brenton will make it. (She has to. Her DNA is programmed for a long life of pom-poms.) I know Cami and Alli will make it. Then there're the other two girls from AlliCam's homeroom, Jackie Swanson and McKenzie Sanford. They're the kind of girls who have their picture in the dictionary next to the defini- tion of pom-pom girls with their perfect hair, skinny jeans, and toothpaste-commercial-white teeth.

That leaves the sixth spot for me, BUT:

A) What if I have an off day? (There are at least ten other girls trying out. They could all be having an "on" day.)

B) What if one of the other girls trying out is better than me?

Big Fat C) What if I don't make it?!!!!

THE COMMENTS OLD HAWK WROTE ON MY VOCABULARY ASSIGNMENT

Dear Abigail,

Your vocabulary sentences lack the following: creativity, proper punctuation, proper grammar, and most of all, effort. Not too many years ago, your mother was an outstanding student for me. I am expecting the same from you this year! Please rewrite this assignment.

Miss Hendrick

TWO THINGS I'M BEGINNING TO REALIZE ABOUT OLD HAWK

1. Up until now, my perfect handwriting and neat, on-time assignments helped me get okay grades. Maybe even grades that were better than I deserved, but it didn't look like this was going to work with Old Hawk. I guess even the neatest paper wasn't going to fool her.

2. Sixth-grade LA was going to be hard.

THE NOTE I WISHED I COULD WRITE TO OLD HAWK

Dear Miss H,

Do you have any idea what my life will be lacking if I don't make pom-poms? How about purpose? How about popularity? How about a reason to live?

I'm putting forth LOTS of effort, but I can't waste it on vocabulary assignments. All you adults think being a kid is so easy, but you should try it. Sixth grade is a lot more stressful than it looks: pom-pom tryouts getting closer by the minute, a friendly letter partner who's the school's biggest outcast, a homeroom teacher who's notorious for being strict (no offense, Miss H, but it's true), and my two best friends in a different homeroom.

Now can you understand why my vocabulary assignment wasn't more important?

Your stressed-out, struggling student,

Abigail

ONE MORE REASON TO HATE THE FRIENDLY LETTER ASSIGNMENT

Old Hawk told us to go home tonight and turn an old shoebox into a mailbox to use when we exchange letters. Where am I? Kindergarten?

The only explanation: Old Hawk regrets never having taught kindergarten and wants to experience it before she dies.

THINGS TO DO FOR LA

1. Rewrite my vocab sentences. (Note to self: this time actually find out what the vocab words mean before writing the sentences.)

2. Make a shoebox-mailbox. (Note to self: look for the craft box full of glue, glitter, sequins, and scissors I used to take with me when I babysat.)

TWO REASONS I DIDN'T MIND MAKING A SHOEBOX-MAILBOX AFTER ALL

1. Old Hawk didn't assign any new LA homework in order to give us time to make our mailboxes.

2. I kind of had fun making my mailbox. My mom even helped, and it turned out supercute.

ONE THING ALLICAM ASKED ME ON THE BUS WHEN THEY SAW MY SHOEBOX - MAILBOX

What _is_ that thing?

ONE ANSWER I GAVE

Just some lame-o thing Old Hawk had us make for LA.

ONE ANSWER I DIDN'T GIVE

Only the coolest shoebox-mailbox ever.

TWO REASONS LA WITH OLD HAWK MIGHT BE BEARABLE

1. Old Hawk finally tore down the bulletin board paper covering the bookshelves in the back of her classroom. Kids had been making jokes about the bones of overworked sixth-graders being hidden behind that paper, but everyone knew that wasn't true. What <u>was</u> behind the paper were hundreds of books, and they didn't look like the books in other classroom libraries, all torn and tattered—the ones we knew teachers bought at garage sales and used bookstores. These books looked new. They were labeled with tags like humor, adventure, mystery, and historical fiction, and they were so organized it looked like a real library shelf. On the bottom shelves all the way across the back of the classroom were different colored baskets. Each of us saw our name printed on one of them and in each basket was a book. One that Old Hawk said she'd chosen just for us.

2. After letting each of us go get our basket—mine had *Newfangled Fairy Tales: Modern Day Fractured Fairy Tales For Teens* in it—Old Hawk explained that we would get silent reading time every day.

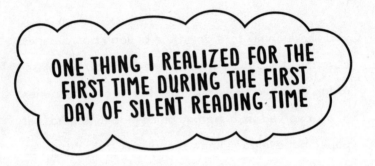

ONE THING I REALIZED FOR THE FIRST TIME DURING THE FIRST DAY OF SILENT READING TIME

All summer, AlliCam and I had been looking at magazines like *Makeover Mania*, *Fashion Hits*, and *Team Spirit*, taking personality and fashion quizzes, reading up on the latest accessories, and finding out the best ways to get middle school boys to notice us. I didn't realize how much I had missed reading a really good book.

ONE THING I ADDED TO MY "WHAT TO BRING HOME FROM SCHOOL TODAY" LIST (RIGHT AFTER "MY MATH BOOK" AND RIGHT BEFORE "MY SCIENCE BOOK")

Newfangled Fairy Tales: Modern Day Fractured Fairy Tales for Teens. (Even though Old Hawk didn't tell us we had to bring it home.)

FRIENDLY LETTER REPLY #1 FROM GABBY TO ME THAT I FOUND IN MY STREAMER, SEQUINED, AND GLITTER-COVERED AWESOMELY CUTE SHOEBOX-MAILBOX

Dear Abby,

Pom-poms? Yeah, I could see that. You're the pom-pom type.

<u>Obviously</u>, you are my letter partner, and <u>obviously</u>, we are both in sixth grade. You're right. I do have an older brother. His name is Pete, but I call him Paul because he's a tree climber. Get it? Paul Bunyan, the lumberjack from the tall tale. Pizza is my favorite food too, but I only like chocolate cake if it has nuts in it. As for *Ella Enchanted*, it was okay, but you've got to be kidding about *Hatchet*. My dad and I <u>loved</u> that book. As for mushrooms, I'm no dummy. I wouldn't eat them if my life depended on it. They could be poisonous. And pumpkin pie? I can take it or leave it.

Looking forward to your next letter.

Your friendly letter friend,
Gabby

THE NOT-SO-FRIENDLY LETTER I WISHED I COULD WRITE TO GABBY

Dear Gabby,

For your information, my name is "Abigail," not "Abby"!

Second of all, I'm not surprised you like the book *Hatchet*. You seem like the *Hatchet* "type." And why would your dad even read it? Sounds a little weird to me.

But most importantly, the reason you can see me as a pom-pom girl is because I was born to be one.

And by the way, calling your brother "Paul" when his name is "Pete" sounds pretty stupid to me, even if he is a tree climber, whatever that is.

Your "Assigned" Letter Partner,

Abigail

THE FRIENDLY LETTER I ACTUALLY PUT IN GABBY'S SHOEBOX - MAILBOX, WHICH SHE HAD DECORATED TO LOOK LIKE A CARTON OF LEMONADE, WHICH MADE NO SENSE (BUT FOR GABBY, MAKING NO SENSE MADE PERFECT SENSE, SO I GUESS FOR HER IT ACTUALLY MADE SENSE)

Dear Gabby,

It's bad enough we have to write these letters, now Old Hawk has us making mailboxes out of shoeboxes? I mean, didn't we all make enough Valentine mailboxes when we were in grade school? Doesn't Old Hawk realize we're almost teenagers?

Speaking of teenagers, how old is your brother? I think he might be in the same grade as my brother, Ben. Ben's a senior and is the captain of the baseball team. He's really good. When I was little, he tried to teach me to play. All I remember about it is he kept saying, "You throw like a girl!" What a stupid thing to say. I AM a girl!

You said your brother's a tree climber. Is that a new extreme sport? I've never heard of it.

Sincerely,
Abigail (NOT Abby!)

P.S. Obviously, I ignored the sarcastic way you used "obviously." But I CANNOT ignore you calling me Abby. My name is ABIGAIL!

ONE HILARIOUS THING THAT HAPPENED AT ALLI'S HOUSE AFTER SCHOOL

We got into World War III with Alli's brother, Brian.

We call Brian "The Brain," because all he ever does is study. And as usual, he was upstairs studying while we were trying to practice poms.

"Turn down that music, you little 'pom freaks'!" he yelled from his bedroom.

Alli's mom wasn't home, so he knew he couldn't get in trouble for yelling at us. Alli's mom would've stuck up for us because she had been a pom-pom girl in high school. She knew how important practicing was.

"Leave us alone!" Alli yelled.

That's when the war started.

First, The Brain threw a pair of balled-up sweat socks

down the stairs at us. We cracked up because he missed us by a mile. (The Brain was <u>really</u> smart but not athletic <u>at all</u>.)

Then Alli threw a bunch of little pillows from the couch. Every pillow she threw hit The Brain. One nailed him right on the forehead.

He threw a few more pairs of socks, which barely made it to the family room, and then he threw a pillow from his bed. The pillow was way too big to throw, so it didn't even make it down the stairs.

Cami and I fell on the floor laughing while Alli grabbed a couple more things to throw. She whipped one of their dog's tennis balls and hit The Brain right in the thigh.

"Ouch!" he yelled and slammed his door.

That's when Alli's dad walked in. He was home early. Cami and I got up from the floor, and Alli dropped the rest of her ammunition, mostly dog toys.

"Oh, hi, Dad!" Alli said, a little out of breath. "We were just going out to the garage to practice. We don't want our music to disturb Brian."

Cami and I followed Alli out into the garage, where the three of us fell on top of each other laughing.

That's when Alli got her brainstorm. A perfect way to get back at The Brain for being such a pain.

In the garage, there was a recycling bin overflowing with newspaper. Instead of practicing poms, we spent the next hour crinkling up newspaper and stuffing it into The Brain's Volkswagen. When we were finished, you couldn't even see inside the car anymore.

Then Alli yelled into the house, "Dad, could you tell Brian it's time for him to drive Cami and Abigail home!"

And the only thing funnier than the look on The Brain's face when he saw his car was the fact that he actually had a red mark on his leg where the tennis ball had hit him.

A NOTE I FOUND IN MY LOCKER AFTER FOURTH PERIOD

Abigail,

At lunch we heard that last year's poms are going to Chitchat after school. It's our chance to get in good with the pom crowd. We HAVE to go!

We'll get off at Cami's stop and walk from there.

Write back!

SPF,
AlliCam

P.S. Jackie and McKenzie are meeting us there.

THREE THINGS I THOUGHT ABOUT DURING SOCIAL STUDIES

1. How much trouble I'd get into for going to Chitchat without permission. (My mom thought I was going to Cami's house to practice after school. The rule was no changing after-school plans during the school day because my mom didn't want me calling her at work all the time asking if I could go here or there.)

2. How supernervous I was! This was really it! Hanging out with <u>real</u> pom-pom girls.

3. Jackie and McKenzie? I worried about homeroom inside jokes. Was I going to spend the whole afternoon feeling left out?

FIVE QUESTIONS I THOUGHT OF THAT GAVE ME A STOMACHACHE BY THE END OF SOCIAL STUDIES

1. Would Jackie and McKenzie like me?

2. Would the other pom girls like me?

3. Would I be able to think of anything to say?

4. Would there be any boys there?

5. Were Alli and Cami as nervous as I was?

THE NOTE I PUT IN ALLICAM'S LOCKER AFTER FIFTH PERIOD

Chitchat with the poms, really? I'm in! See you on the bus!

SPF,

Abigail

SOMETHING WE DID ON THE BUS ON THE WAY TO CHITCHAT

AlliCam and I took turns brushing each other's hair. We wanted to make sure we looked perfect when we got there. The problem was, AlliCam's hair already looked good before we even started, and mine didn't look much better when we were finished.

Thankfully, Alli had a great idea. She put one little braid on each side of my hair and used a hair clip to pull them together in the back. I checked it out in the mirror that Cami kept in her backpack, and it looked sort of like a style you'd see in a magazine.

By the time we got there, AlliCam looked like they belonged on the pom squad, and I hoped I did too.

FIVE THINGS THAT HAPPENED AT CHITCHAT

1. As soon as we saw Jackie and McKenzie in the parking lot, they both yelled, "Hello, daaaaarlings!" And AlliCam both yelled the same thing to them, <u>exactly</u> the same way. It must've been a homeroom thing. I cringed. Feeling left out with AlliCam was bad enough, but with AlliCam and J&M it was going to be unbearable.

2. Inside, we ordered at the counter, and while we waited for our food, we saw the seventh- and eighth-grade poms sitting in the corner booth. One of the poms recognized Jackie and Alli from the pom practice session last summer, so they called us over. I wondered why they didn't recognize me. Maybe Cami and McKenzie were wondering the same thing.

3. The other girls invited us to sit down with them, but there was only room for four more in their booth. AlliCam and J&M got those four spots, so guess who had to pull up a chair? This wouldn't have been so bad except the booth

was higher than the tables, so my chair was too low. I felt like I was a little kid sitting at the adults' table.

4. I tried to make the best of it, but it's hard to join in the conversation when your chin is almost resting on the table. Besides that, I couldn't think of anything interesting to say. AlliCam and J&M were all, "I love that eye shadow," and "How do you get your hair so shiny?" Blah, blah, blah. The older girls were loving all the attention and compliments.

5. The worst and the best parts happened when the boys showed up. They came over and crowded around our booth. All I could smell was cologne. It made me woozy, so I couldn't concentrate on the conversation. It made it impossible to think of anything to say, let alone something interesting, funny, or smart.

Since I was sitting on the end of the booth, the boys crowded around me.

This should've been a good thing; but somehow, maybe because of that stupid low chair, not one guy even noticed I was there. I felt like a bug that could've easily been swatted away, or worse yet, squashed to smithereens.

ONE THING TO DO BEFORE HANGING OUT WITH THE POMS AGAIN

Make a list of interesting things to say to the seventh- and eighth-grade poms.

THREE REASONS I'M BEGINNING TO BE FURIOUS WITH ALLICAM

1. I'm <u>so</u> sick of their inside jokes I'm ready to puke. This morning on the bus, they were doing some sort of sign language thing—hand signals and shrugging their shoulders at each other. Then doubling over in fits of laughter. I didn't know <u>what</u> they were doing.

"C'mon, you guys, cut it out!" I said.

But they wouldn't stop.

"Oh, Abigail, just chill out! We're only goofing around," Alli said as both of them broke down in another fit of laughter. I was hoping they'd laugh so hard they'd pee their pants.

When they headed off to homeroom, I felt like giving <u>them</u> a hand signal that I'd get grounded for if anyone saw it.

2. AlliCam kept talking about how great it was to practice with Jackie and McKenzie at lunchtime. They know I don't have anyone to practice with at lunch. The only girls in my homeroom who are trying out are Jeannie and Marcy. And for obvious reasons, they're not exactly pom-pom girl material. You'd think AlliCam would be a little more loyal. I mean, after all, we're supposed to be best friends and sisters.

3. But the biggest reason I'm furious with AlliCam is because of what happened at my house. They slept over Friday night, and we'd stayed up really late doing makeovers, making a list of all the cute boys in middle school, watching TV, baking cookies, and painting each other's toenails.

About four a.m., we finally crawled into our sleeping bags. We whispered to each other for a few minutes in the dark, and eventually AlliCam started talking about stuff that happened in homeroom, so I just lay quietly listening. I was quiet for so long, I guess they thought I was asleep because pretty soon they started talking about me.

"Do you wish we'd gone to McKenzie's house tonight instead of coming here?" Alli asked.

"I don't know," Cami answered. "Do you?"

"I don't know," Alli said. "I'm dying to see her house. Jackie says it's like a mansion...but this was fun too."

"Jackie told me they were going to practice the pom routine with McKenzie's older sister. She's on varsity poms at Westdale High."

"I know. That would've been great," Alli said.

"I just can't believe how supercool and fun McKenzie and Jackie are," Cami said, yawning. "We're so lucky the four of us ended up in the same homeroom. Sixth grade is turning out to be awesome."

"Totally," agreed Alli. "When the four of us make poms, it's going to be great."

"You mean the five of us." Cami sighed. "Don't forget about Abigail."

"Oh, yeah, Abigail too," Alli mumbled, as they both rolled over and said, "G'night," to each other.

Don't forget Abigail?! How could they forget me? We were SPF. I squeezed my eyes shut really tight hoping to keep the tears from coming out.

ONE THING THAT HAPPENED AS I LAY IN THE DARK LISTENING TO ALLICAM SLEEP

Tears slid sideways onto my pillow until I had to turn it over because it was so wet.

ONE THING MY DAD DID SATURDAY MORNING AFTER ALLICAM LEFT

Took me out for doughnuts, just him and me, even though I wouldn't tell him what was wrong.

SOMETHING THAT HAPPENED SATURDAY AFTERNOON THAT ALMOST MADE ME FORGET WHAT I'D HEARD ALLICAM SAY

Alli called to tell me that her dad had gotten three movie passes from one of his golfing buddies. The passes were about to expire, and the guy couldn't use them. Alli's dad said he'd drive us if we wanted to go see something. Cami's mom had already said yes, and I knew my mom would say yes too.

The only thing I didn't know was whether Alli would've called me if her dad had gotten <u>four</u> movie passes instead of <u>three</u>.

ONE WEIRD THING THAT HAPPENED AT THE MOVIES

When I went out to the lobby to use the bathroom before the movie started, I saw Jackson Dawber standing in the popcorn line with his older brother Max and one of Max's friends.

Everyone knew Max had just gotten back from a summer at some boot camp for bad kids. Last year he was only a freshman, but already he'd threatened the school secretary when she gave him a detention for his tenth tardy, gotten suspended for starting a food fight in the cafeteria, and gotten kicked off the baseball team for swearing at his coach during a game. The principal told his parents if he didn't go to the boot camp, he couldn't come back to high school. But from what I saw, camping out with the bad kids hadn't done much good. Max and his friend were pelting Jackson with pennies and kind of shoving him around. They thought they were being funny, but I could tell by the look on

Jackson's face that he wasn't having any fun. I ducked into the bathroom before Jackson saw me.

I would've forgotten the whole thing except on Monday morning, when I got on the bus, Jackson was throwing goldfish crackers at a little second-grader sitting in the seat across from him. What a jerk! Why would he pick on someone when he knew what it felt like to be teased like that? Jackson was an even bigger jerk than I thought.

FRIENDLY LETTER REPLY #2

Dear Abby (oh, sorry, I mean Abigail),

We should give Old Hawk a break. So what if she makes us decorate mailboxes? It beats diagramming sentences. I think it would be fun to secretly make a mailbox for her. Then write letters to her anonymously and stick them inside. What do you think?

Tree climbing is NOT an extreme sport. It's a job. My brother would be a senior this year, but he dropped out of school to work. He climbs trees and cuts them down for people. It's a dangerous job, but he's really good at it. He says he loves climbing around in the tree branches like a raccoon.

As for baseball, I think I've seen your brother play. He's the pitcher, right? That's why he says you throw like a girl. He probably thinks anyone who doesn't throw the ball a hundred miles an hour throws like a girl. I bet if he tried to climb a tree, my brother would tell him he climbs like a girl.

Talk to you later,

Gabby

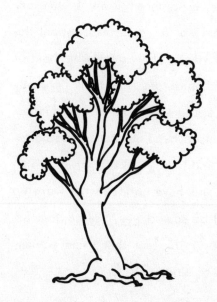

THREE REASONS I'M REALLY GETTING NERVOUS ABOUT POM TRYOUTS

1. On my way to science class today I saw Cami, Alli, Jackie, and McKenzie practicing the pom-pom routine. They might as well start calling themselves the Laker Girls. All four of them were shaking their hips faster than a hula girl at a luau.

2. Jeannie and Marcy asked me to practice with them at lunch. I couldn't really say no since I sit with them every day, so I said yes. That was a big mistake. I spent the entire lunch period trying to show them what beat of the music the routine starts on. They think I'm really good. The problem is Old Hawk shaking the feather duster she uses to clean her bookshelves would be better than Jeannie and Marcy. (Okay, that's an exaggeration.) But these girls have no idea what we're up against. They should be scared, very scared. Instead, they're all gah-gah over the fact that I can actually remember the whole routine.

3. THE POM-POM PRINCESS Alicia NEVER practices. She doesn't have to. Because of her sister, she's a legend in her own time. All she has to do is show up to tryouts. And she knows it. Her overwhelming confidence is causing me to hyperventilate with hopelessness.

THINGS TO DO TONIGHT

1. Practice poms.
2. Cross fingers AND toes.
3. Repeat.

THREE REASONS WHY I HATE RIDING THE BUS

1. AlliCam are <u>really</u> getting on my nerves. I don't even want to sit with them anymore. This must be what it's like to have <u>real</u> sisters.

   Besides all the inside jokes, they keep talking about funny stuff that happened in class and then turning to me and saying, "Sorry, Abigail. Guess you <u>had</u> to be there."

   Or they talk about their e-mail pen pals from Paris, France. Of course, Mr. Blue Eyes, being the cool new teacher that he is, is totally into computers and the Internet for LA assignments. So while I'm stuck writing old-fashioned friendly letters to Gabby Marco of Crestdale Heights, they're e-mailing two French girls named Brigitte and Colette, who are practically supermodels. (I saw the photos they e-mailed. Both are definitely born for the runway.)

   And I won't even mention how much they talk about J&M. I'm so sick of them, and I barely even know them. What's it going to be like when we're all on poms together?

2. Jackson Dawber started making fun of Gabby yesterday. He found out that Gabby calls her brother "Paul Bunyan," so he started calling her Babe the Blue Ox. (I don't know how he found out about the Paul Bunyan thing. I didn't tell him, but I think I might've mentioned it to AlliCam. I can't believe they'd tell Jackson, but maybe they did. I felt kind of crummy thinking that I might've been the reason Jackson was calling her Babe.)

While Jackson was being his normal idiotic self, Gabby just sat there in her usual seat in the middle of the bus staring out the window. I did see her close her eyes and take a deep breath, but otherwise, she acted like she couldn't even hear Jackson singing at the top of his lungs.

"Old Paul Bunyan had an ox.
E-I-E-I-O.
And that old ox was big and blue.
E-I-E-I-O.
With a Gabby, Gabby here;
And a Gabby, Gabby there..."

I swear that kid is so demented sometimes.

Why was Jackson such a moron when he really should've known better?

3. The day after the Paul Bunyan thing, when Gabby got on the bus, she pulled something out of a plastic bag. She held it up for me to see. Thankfully, AlliCam were comparing their nail polish color at the time and didn't notice. It was a shoebox decorated like a hawk. The thing had feathers all over it, a big old hawk head, and a hook beak. She'd made a mailbox for Miss Hendrick and decorated it like a hawk! Was she crazy?

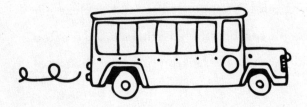

THE NOTE I SLIPPED TO GABBY BEFORE HOMEROOM

Dear Gabby,

Are you nuts? What do you think Old Hawk is going to say when she sees that thing on her desk? You must want to get suspended or something. You better not say I had anything to do with it.

Abigail

THE SPEECH OLD HAWK GAVE US IN LA BEFORE SHE NOTICED THE OLD HAWK MAILBOX ON HER DESK

"These spelling papers are astonishingly atrocious, my friends!" she said, shaking a stack of notebook paper at us.

The papers had so much red ink all over them that they looked like blood-splattered evidence from a crime scene.

"I have to call a spade a spade here and say that this is simply not sixth-grade work."

I knew half the class was thinking, "What the heck does a spade have to do with spelling papers?" The other half was thinking, "What in the world is a spade?"

Old Hawk went on with her sermon. "Furthermore, I am not accustomed, and will never be accustomed, to accepting this kind of work! Now the burning question of the day is, what are we going to do about this?"

No one moved a muscle. No one coughed. No one

scratched an itch. No one even blinked an eye for fear Old Hawk would think they had an answer to her question.

I kept thinking if the question were really "burning," every fire alarm in the whole school would've been going off because NO ONE was going to answer Old Hawk.

THE THING OLD HAWK SAID WHEN SHE NOTICED HER NEW MAILBOX

"Good heavens! What on earth is this?"

THE NOTE OLD HAWK PULLED OUT OF HER NEW MAILBOX

Dear Miss Hendrick,

We've been having so much fun exchanging friendly letters. We didn't want you to feel left out, so here's a mailbox for you. It's decorated like a hawk because hawks like to sit on perches and watch over things just like you sit on your stool and watch over us while you teach.

Enjoy your mail!

Sincerely,
Spirit of the Sixth-Grade Sky

THE REASON WHY EVERYONE IS GOING TO WRITE LETTERS AND PUT THEM IN THE OLD HAWK MAILBOX

After reading Gabby's letter, Old Hawk was flying high. She sat on her stool during language arts smiling like a proud peacock fanning her feathers. I didn't even know she <u>could</u> smile.

She let us quit our vocabulary practice five minutes early so we could talk quietly with our friends until the bell rang. That's when I heard kids whispering about writing her nice notes all the time to keep her in a good mood every day.

Someone said, "Whoever came up with the mailbox idea is a genius."

I looked over at Gabby. As usual, she had her head in a book and was laughing to herself in her usual weird way. I wondered what everyone would think if they knew Gabby was the one who had made the mailbox.

THE REASON I FEEL LIKE THROWING UP THIS MORNING

Pom-pom tryouts are TODAY.

THE POST-IT NOTE I FOUND ON THE BATHROOM MIRROR WHEN I GOT OUT OF THE SHOWER

Abigail,

Just do your best, and you'll knock 'em dead, sweetie!

♥

Mom (& Dad)

THE REASON WHY I'M FREAKING OUT ABOUT POM-POM TRYOUTS

I'm sooooo tired. I lay in bed last night going over and over the pom-pom routine in my mind. The last time I looked at my clock it said 3:17 a.m. When my alarm went off at seven, I felt like I hadn't slept at all. My brain feels like mushy oatmeal. (And thinking about oatmeal makes me want to throw up even more.) I'm so stressed, I don't think I can even remember the routine. If I don't make the pom squad...I'm so freaked out I can't even think of words to describe how horrific my life will be if I don't make it.

THINGS TO DO TO STAY CALM TODAY

1. Take deep breaths.
2. Read Post-it note from Mom and Dad.
3. Repeat.

THE NOTE GABBY SLIPPED TO ME BEFORE HOMEROOM

Dear Abigail,

Miss H is in Old Hawk heaven with that mailbox. She's too happy to wonder who made it for her, so you don't have to worry. I think it'll work out pretty well for the whole class.

Gabby

P.S. I know you have pom tryouts today. I don't get why anyone would want to jump around on a basketball court, shaking fistfuls of colored paper streamers in front of a huge crowd. Especially wearing those short skirts and tight sequined tops, but hey, whatever. Everybody has their thing. I know you really want to make it, so good luck. Shake it like you mean it!

♥

THE REASON WHY GABBY REALLY BUGS ME

She's acting like she's Little Miss I'm-Above-Being-a-Pom-Pom-Girl. I'm sure she's just jealous because she knows <u>she</u> couldn't be one if her life depended on it. There's more chance of Old Hawk being voted students' favorite teacher than of Gabby making the pom-pom squad.

THREE GOOD THINGS ABOUT TRYOUTS/THREE BAD THINGS ABOUT TRYOUTS

1. We got to do our routine in groups of threes. AlliCam and I got to be a group. ☺

   I could tell by the way the judges smiled at AlliCam that they liked them better than me. ☹

2. I did my cartwheels and roundoffs perfectly. ☺

   So did everyone else. ☹

3. The seventh- and eighth-graders who were watching told me <u>I</u> was awesome. ☺

   They told <u>everyone</u> they were awesome. ☹

THE REASON I WON'T BE ABLE TO SLEEP AGAIN TONIGHT

Before homeroom tomorrow, the pom-pom squad roster will be posted outside the office.

THE NOTE I FOUND ON THE KITCHEN COUNTER IN THE MORNING, NEXT TO A CHOCOLATE GLAZED DOUGHNUT

Abs,

Had to leave early this morning.
  Toes and fingers crossed for you today!
  Love you no matter what!

Dad

THE ROSTER POSTED
OUTSIDE THE OFFICE READ

1. Cami Anderson
2. Alicia Brenton
3. Alli Martin
4. McKenzie Sanford
5. Jackie Swanson
6. *Abigail Walters

THREE REASONS I'M FLYING HIGHER THAN OLD HAWK

1. I MADE IT!!!!!

2. AlliCam made it! SISTERS POMS FOREVER!!!

3. Jackie and McKenzie said that maybe the star by my name means that they've chosen me as the sixth-grade captain. Maybe Jackie and McKenzie aren't as bad as I thought. Now that we're all on poms together, I bet the five of us will get along great.

And I can't believe it! Me! The captain? I couldn't be more excited if I were going to Hollywood on *American Idol*.

FRIENDLY LETTER #3
FROM ME TO GABBY

Dear Gabby,

Thanks for wishing me luck. I'm sure you've heard by now that I made the pom squad. It looks like I might even be the sixth-grade captain. I know you don't think it's any big deal, but being a pom-pom girl is one of the greatest accomplishments for a middle school girl. It changes people's lives. And being the captain is like landing the starring role in a major motion picture. It's hard to imagine it's all happening to me.

Abigail Walters
Pom-Pom Girl (Waiting to be named captain)

P.S. Way to go with the mailbox! Old Hawk's been a dream lately, thanks to you.

THREE REASONS I LOVE BEING A POM-POM GIRL

1. Kip Thompson. He said hi to me in the hall. He's one of THE cutest guys in the entire seventh grade. He's never even <u>looked</u> at me, let alone talked to me before today, so it HAS to be because of poms.

2. The secret wave. AlliCam and I spent the entire bus ride coming up with an idea for a secret pom-pom girl wave. Something all us pom girls can do when we pass each other in the hall. The one we decided on is <u>so</u> cute. We salute each other with our right hand and then slide our hand down the side of our head and wave with two fingers. Since I'm going to be the sixth-grade captain, I'm going to suggest the new wave to the eighth-grade captain at our first practice.

3. Our pom-pom girl uniforms. Tomorrow is our first practice. We get to try on our new uniforms. I know once I put on that skirt and those sequins, my life is <u>never</u> going to be the same.

BEFORE SCHOOL THE NEXT DAY I FOUND THIS NOTE TAPED TO MY LOCKER

Abigail Walters,

Please come see me in my office before school.

Coach Jenson

THREE QUESTIONS I HAVE ABOUT THE NOTE

1. Why does the note have yesterday's date on it?

2. Does Ms. Jenson want to tell me that I've been named sixth-grade captain?

3. Why does she want to see me <u>before</u> school when our first practice is <u>after</u> school?

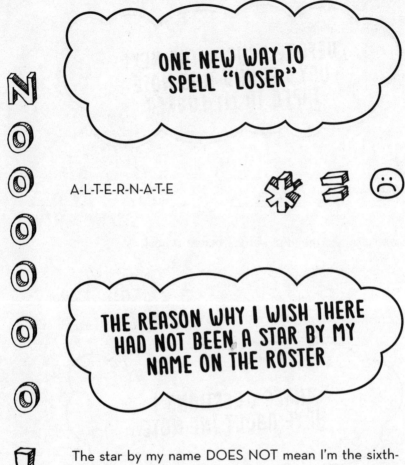

ONE NEW WAY TO SPELL "LOSER"

A-L-T-E-R-N-A-T-E

THE REASON WHY I WISH THERE HAD NOT BEEN A STAR BY MY NAME ON THE ROSTER

The star by my name DOES NOT mean I'm the sixth-grade captain. It means I didn't really make the squad. It means I'm an ALTERNATE.

Ms. Jenson explained that, this year, they had decided to cut the sixth-grade squad to five girls so that they could add more girls to the eighth-grade squad. "We think it's important to give the eighth-graders more opportunities since it's their last year of middle school," Ms. Jenson said.

More opportunities for eighth-graders? What? Everyone knew that sixth-graders were the ones who needed more opportunities. We were the ones struggling to survive middle school for the very first time in our lives.

Ms. Jenson went on to explain that being an alternate meant that if someone couldn't fulfill their commitment to the squad (she should've said fulfill their dream of a <u>lifetime</u>) then I would get to take their place. All I could think was that being an alternate for a pom-pom girl at Crestdale Heights was like being an alternate for someone who wins the lottery.

"Oh, I'm sorry, I really don't want this million dollars. You take it instead. I hate spending money, so go ahead and have it."

Being an alternate meant NEVER being a pom-pom girl.

Ms. Jenson blabbed on and on about how she had wanted to tell me this yesterday and that she didn't know why I didn't get the note until today. While she talked, I thought about how instead of "alternate" she should've just said if there's a star by your name, it means "you have no <u>chance</u> of being popular" and "forget about Kip Thompson ever talking to you again."

TEN REASONS I WISH I WERE SOMEONE ELSE

1. I am NOT a pom-pom girl.
2. Ditto
3. Ditto
4. Ditto
5. Ditto
6. Ditto
7. Ditto
8. Ditto
9. Ditto
10. Ditto

THREE THINGS I DID AFTER TALKING TO MS. JENSON

1. I went to find AlliCam.

2. I took them into the bathroom.

3. I said, "I'm not a pom-pom girl. I'm an alternate." Then I bawled my eyes out. Neither of them knew what to do. Somehow that made me feel worse.

> # THE THING I THOUGHT ABOUT DURING FIRST PERIOD WHILE I HID MY BLOTCHY FACE AND RED EYES BEHIND MY READING BOOK

What about SPF? Without the "P" would there be an "S" and "F"?

> # QUESTIONS I THOUGHT ABOUT LATER IN THE DAY

Would I be in the pom squad yearbook photo listed as an alternate? Or would I not be in it at all? I didn't know which one was worse.

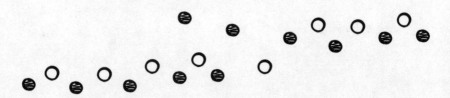

THREE REASONS I'M GOING TO <u>HAVE TO</u> GET A NEW LIFE

1. Today AlliCam stayed after school for their first pom-pom practice, so I had to sit alone on the bus.

2. Gabby kept looking up from the book she had her head buried in to stare at me. She better not even <u>think</u> about trying to sit with me just because AlliCam aren't around. I have enough problems without being associated with <u>her</u> freakishness.

3. After school I watched TV Land reruns and ate ten 100-calorie snack bags—three Oreos, four Cheese Nips, and three Lorna Doones. If I kept this up, everyone might start calling me "Flabby Abby."

ONE THING MY MOM DID

Let me eat dinner in my room.

ONE THING MY DAD DID

Brought me my dessert.

ONE THING MY BROTHER DID

Opened my bedroom door, stuck his head in, and said,

"They don't know what they're missin'."

ONE THING I DID

Cried even harder because even though they all were
being so nice to me, it didn't make me feel any better.

THE REASON I MAY HAVE TO SWITCH SCHOOLS

AlliCam taught the whole pom-pom squad the secret wave (which was <u>my</u> idea). Every time I go into the hall, I see them saluting and wiggling their fingers at each other. How could something I thought was so cute yesterday make me want to cry so hard today?

THE NOTE MISS HENDRICK PULLED OUT OF HER OLD HAWK MAILBOX TODAY

Roses are red

Violets are blue

The kids in 6H

Are glad we got YOU!

THE REASON WHY EVERYONE KNEW THE NOTE WAS FROM JACKSON DAWBER

No one else would write something so <u>stupid</u>.

THREE REASONS WHY EVERYONE THINKS JACKSON'S STUPID POEM IS GENIUS

1. Old Hawk let us work in groups today for spelling, <u>and</u> we got to pick our own groups.
2. She shortened our homework assignment from ten questions to five.
3. She ended language arts ten minutes early so she could start reading *Tuck Everlasting*.

THREE REASONS WHY EVEN OLD HAWK'S GOOD MOOD DIDN'T CHEER ME UP

1. Being able to choose my own group didn't do me any good since AlliCam aren't in my class. I ended up working with Jeannie and Marcy, but that just made me feel like a "pom-pom girl loser" because they tried out and didn't make it either.

2. Having less homework just meant I'd have <u>more</u> time after school to watch reruns and eat junk food. Not that I like homework or anything. I'm not <u>that</u> much of a geek—not yet anyway, but I already didn't have enough to do after school.

3. I couldn't enjoy *Tuck Everlasting* because right before Old Hawk started reading it, a note came for me from the office.

Dear Abigail,

Every Thursday, I'd like you to join the pom squad's practice.
That way you'll know the routines if you ever have to fill in.
  We'll start tomorrow!

                              See you then!
                              Ms. Jenson

ONE THING I THOUGHT ABOUT AFTER READING MS. JENSON'S NOTE

At least I'd get to hang out with the poms one day a
week. That was something.

> ## ONE QUESTION I DIDN'T WANT TO THINK ABOUT BECAUSE I ALREADY KNEW THE ANSWER

Would that be enough to make me part of the pom crowd?

> ## THE ANSWER I ALREADY KNEW

<u>NO.</u>

> ## THE WORST THING ABOUT BEING AN ALTERNATE FOR THE POM SQUAD

Still feeling like you're not a real pom-pom girl.

> ### THREE THINGS THAT HAPPENED AT POM PRACTICE THAT MADE ME REALIZE THAT GOING TO PRACTICE WAS THE WORST PART OF BEING AN ALTERNATE

1. All the girls—that is all the girls except me—had matching "POMS FOREVER" T-shirts that Jackie's mom had specially made for them.

2. They were learning a new routine, and even though <u>everyone</u> kept making mistakes, Jackie kept acting like I was the only one messing up. She kept putting her hand on her hip, sighing, and then rolling her eyes at me.

3. At break time, AlliCam totally ignored me because they were so busy listening to J&M talk about a new girl in their homeroom who, as they put it, must be from "the last train to Loserville."

    "She actually wore overalls the other day," Jackie said, while pretending to gag herself with one finger. "Who does she think she is? Farmer Fran? This isn't 4-H camp."

    She cracked her gum for about the hundredth time. All the other girls laughed, but for some reason, it didn't sound that funny to me.

ONE WAY TO DESCRIBE BEING AN ALTERNATE AT PRACTICE

Like low-fat frozen yogurt compared to real chocolate ice cream. No, make that a scoop of lumpy, disgusting cottage cheese compared to an extra large hot fudge sundae topped with homemade whipped cream—nothing about it is the same.

THE ONE THING THAT WOULD MAKE THAT LUMPY, DISGUSTING COTTAGE CHEESE TASTE LIKE IT WAS SPRINKLED WITH DIRT

Being in the pom squad yearbook photo, not dressed in a uniform, and listed as an alternate—and I was afraid this was going to be my *destiny*.

ONE THING I WAS THANKFUL FOR

I wouldn't have to go back to pom practice for a whole week.

ONE THING I WANTED TO DO AFTER PRACTICE

Talk to AlliCam about how bad I felt.

ONE REASON I DIDN'T

I'm not sure they cared, and that made me feel worse.

THE NOTE MISS HENDRICK PULLED OUT OF HER OLD HAWK MAILBOX FRIDAY MORNING

Dear Miss Hendrick,

We love exchanging friendly letters! Thank you for giving us this opportunity to communicate with our peers using our writing.

Since we're enjoying it so much, maybe the friendly letter partners should spend some time together. How about partner spelling practice or partner vocabulary sentence review? If we get to know our partners better, we'll probably have more things to write about.

Sincerely,
Sixth-Grade Spirit in the Sky

FOUR THINGS OLD HAWK SAID AFTER READING THE LETTER

1. "What a <u>marvelous</u> idea!"

2. "See how much the English language, when used properly, brings people together, my friends?"

3. "All that text messaging and IMing has left this generation starved for good old-fashioned written communication."

4. "Let's make this partner day, shall we? Please push your desks together and spend the entire class period getting to know one another better."

(She said all four things with that HUGE smile she's had on her face ever since Gabby gave her that insanely <u>stupid</u> mailbox.)

109

THREE THINGS I WAS THINKING AFTER OLD HAWK'S PDA (PUBLIC DISPLAY OF APPRECIATION)

1. I have to spend the entire language arts period with my desk pushed up next to Gabby's?

2. Isn't my life miserable enough already?

3. I'm going to kill Gabby for writing that note to Old Hawk.

ONE THING I'M SURE THE REST OF THE CLASS WAS THINKING WHILE THEY PUSHED THEIR DESKS NEXT TO THEIR FRIENDLY LETTER PARTNERS

Who cares who my partner is?! This whole period is going to be a BLOW OFF!!!!

ONE THING EVERYONE DID WITH THEIR PARTNERS

T-A-L-K-E-D for the <u>whole</u> forty minutes.

HERE'S A LIST OF WHAT EVERYONE TALKED ABOUT

1. How lame the friendly letter assignment is.
2. How genius the Old Hawk mailbox is.
3. What was on TV last night.
4. How the tuna casserole in the cafeteria must be part cat food to taste as bad as it does.
5. What movies were showing this weekend.
6. What movies just came out for rental.
7. How great it is to get to talk with partners for the whole class period. (The only thing better is watching a movie.)

ONE THING I HEARD JACKSON ASK BRENT ONCE ALL OUR DESKS WERE PUSHED NEXT TO OUR PARTNERS

"Don't Abigail and Gabby look cute together?"

ONE QUESTION I WANTED TO ASK THE WHOLE CLASS

Is there anyone more annoying than Jackson Dawber?

ONE THING BRENT SAID TO JACKSON TO ANSWER HIS QUESTION ABOUT GABBY AND ME

"They're perfect for each other."

ONE THING I ASKED MYSELF

What does <u>that</u> mean?

ONE THING I OVERHEARD BRENT ASK JACKSON

"You trying out for basketball this year?"

TWO ANSWERS JACKSON GAVE BRENT

1. "No way. Last year I went to conditioning for two weeks, and all the guys were all buddy-buddy the whole time, but then I got cut, and no one on the team even talked to me anymore."

2. "Forget that, man. I got better things to do."

THREE MORE QUESTIONS I HAD

1. Was poms like basketball?
2. What better things did Jackson have to do—think of new ways to make an idiot of himself?
3. Would I have to find better things to do too?

THREE THINGS OLD HAWK WROTE ON THE CHALKBOARD

With Your Partner:

1. Spend ten minutes telling each other three things you've enjoyed about writing friendly letters.
2. Spend fifteen minutes practicing next week's spelling words.
3. Spend fifteen minutes writing next week's vocabulary sentences.

A LIST OF WHAT GABBY SAID AND A LIST OF WHAT I DID WHILE WE SAT NEXT TO EACH OTHER

1. "That Old Hawk mailbox is working out all right, isn't it?"

   I stared at my spiral notebook.

2. "Beats listening to Old Hawk's cute little first-grade spelling tricks for each spelling word, or her ten-minute-long <u>supposedly humorous</u> explanations of each vocabulary word."

   I shrugged my shoulders.

3. "So you must be pretty bummed about poms, huh?"

   I clenched my teeth and stared at Gabby. I wished I could fold up her freakishness, stuff it into an envelope, and mail it to the South Pole. (That was the farthest place I could think of.)

4. "It's not the end of the world, you know."

   That's when all the anger, frustration, and disappointment of my shattered pom-pom girl dreams turned into hot lava. It erupted from me like I was an active volcano.

WHAT HAPPENED WHEN THE VOLCANO ERUPTED

When Gabby said, "It's not the end of the world, you know," I lunged at her like it was Friday night at the fights. I knocked her off her chair and somehow ended up on top of her. Old Hawk swooped down on us before I even realized what I'd done. She pulled me off Gabby like she'd worked in a prison her whole life and breaking up fights was something she did every day.

"What is the meaning of this completely inappropriate outburst, Abigail!"

Gabby jumped up right away and said, "Oh, nothing, Miss Hendrick. Abigail was just showing me this trick she learned in her self-defense class. I'm okay. I asked her to show it to me."

I was in shock. I didn't know what to say. The rest of the class stared at us like we were aliens. Old Hawk looked at us like she didn't believe Gabby. We sat down, and Old Hawk went back to her desk.

FIVE THINGS THAT HAPPENED AFTER I TACKLED GABBY

1. I said, "Thanks," but wondered why Gabby had covered for me.

2. Gabby and I opened our notebooks and, without saying a word, wrote our vocabulary sentences.

3. When Gabby finished her work, she grabbed a grimy paperback sticking out of the pocket of her backpack and cracked it open. It was a copy of *Stone Fox*.

   Mr. Kirby had read it to us last year, so I didn't know why Gabby was reading it again. I noticed there were little stick figure drawings and writing in the margins on almost every page.

4. Five minutes before the bell rang, with her head still buried in her book, Gabby started her usual laughing for no reason. *Stone Fox* wasn't a funny story, so what was she laughing about? She covered her mouth and chuckled to herself for at least a full minute.

5. I let out an exasperated sigh and wondered how

someone could act so normal one minute and so bizarre the next. No wonder Gabby Marco had no friends. It was her own dumb fault.

THE ONE THING GABBY DID ON THE WAY OUT THE DOOR

Pulled out a stack of yellow business cards from her back pocket and stuck one in the palm of my hand.

SHE DOESN'T MAKE SENSE

THE ONE SENTENCE PRINTED ON THE YELLOW BUSINESS CARD

When life hands you lemons, don't pucker and pout, make lemonade and laugh out loud.

Margaret Marco

THE FOUR QUESTIONS I HAD AFTER READING THE CARD

1. What in the world did it mean?
2. Why in the world did Gabby give it to me?
3. Who in the world was Margaret Marco?
4. Was this why Gabby decorated her shoebox-mailbox like a carton of lemonade?

ONE QUESTION MY DAD ASKED AT DINNER

"Anything interesting happen at school today?"

THE ANSWER I GAVE

Shrugged my shoulders and said, "Not really," before I shoved a huge spoonful of mashed potatoes in my mouth.

THE LETTER I FOUND IN MY FRIENDLY LETTER MAILBOX THE NEXT DAY

Abigail,

Yesterday was hilarious! When you tackled me, it probably looked like we planned it as a prank. I think Old Hawk was ready to have a heart attack.

I didn't mean to make you mad, but I meant it when I said, "It's not the end of the world." My mom always used to say that to me. And she was right. She always said that thing about making lemonade from lemons too.

That's why I made the cards—to give them to people who seem like they have a lot of lemons and don't know what to do. Seems like you have a bunch.

Sincerely,
Gabby

ONE THING I WONDERED AFTER I READ GABBY'S LETTER

Where <u>was</u> Gabby's mom?

THE NOTE I PASSED TO GABBY IN SOCIAL STUDIES WHEN I GOT UP TO SHARPEN MY PENCIL

Gabby,

Where is your mom anyway?

Abigail

THE NOTE GABBY DROPPED ON MY DESK WHEN SHE GOT UP TO THROW SOMETHING AWAY

She died when I was in third grade.

ONE THING I FELT AFTER READING GABBY'S NOTE

Awful.

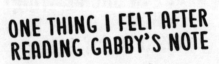

× 100,000,000,000,000

ONE REASON I FELT AWFUL

Knowing Gabby didn't live with her parents didn't seem like a big deal, but knowing her mom was dead made me feel <u>horrible</u>.

THREE THINGS I WONDERED

1. How had Gabby's mom died?
2. Where was Gabby's dad?
3. What did it feel like to be Gabby?

THE TERRIBLE THING THAT HAPPENED ON THE BUS ON THE WAY HOME

When I got on the bus, I saw kids crowded around a seat in the middle of the bus, talking and laughing. It looked like they were standing by the seat where Gabby usually sat. When I got closer, I realized it <u>was</u> Gabby's usual seat, and I saw the words SUMO WRESTLER written on a big piece of construction paper taped to the seat. Even before I spotted Jackson "the idiot boy" Dawber sitting in the back of the bus grinning, I knew who'd done it. I wished I had the guts to slap that grin right off his face.

A minute later, Gabby got on the bus. Everyone froze.

No one said a word until Jackson yelled from the back of the bus, "Introducing Crestdale Heights' homegrown sumo wrestler, better known as Babe the Blue Ox!"

Kids laughed like the audience of a live sitcom.

Gabby didn't move. I didn't either. I don't even think I breathed. I was worried that Jackson might come up with a sumo name for me. After all, I was the one who wrestled Gabby to the ground. And if I kept chowing down on those snack bags every day after school, pretty soon, I might actually be sumo size.

Gabby closed her eyes, pressed her lips together, and took a deep breath. Then thankfully the bus driver came up the steps behind Gabby. Everyone scurried to find seats. Jackson's friend Brent tore off the sumo sign and crumpled it into a ball. Gabby sat in the seat behind the driver, and I sat down next to some fourth-graders a few rows back.

I wondered if Gabby was sorry she had covered for me with Old Hawk. I knew I was sorry that I had found out about Gabby's mom because it only made me feel worse about everything.

127

THE NOTE I LEFT STICKING OUT OF THE POCKET OF MY MOM'S PURSE

Dear Mom,

Thanks for working on my shoebox-mailbox with me.

It never would've turned out so cute without your help.

It was fun!

Abigail

THE REASON WHY WRITING THE NOTE TO MY MOM FELT GOOD AND BAD

Good: because making the mailbox with my mom had been fun, and I hadn't remembered to thank her.

Bad: because it made me think about how Gabby's mom wasn't even around to help her with her lemonade carton mailbox.

AN EVEN WORSE THING THAT HAPPENED ON THE BUS THE NEXT DAY

I was barely awake when we got to Gabby's stop the next morning, but I woke up quickly when Gabby's brother, aka Paul Bunyan, was waiting for the bus with her. He was all scruffy looking with sort of a beard. He wore old work clothes that looked dirty. But nobody paid too much attention to what he looked like because he screamed at all of us, "IF ANYONE <u>EVER</u> MAKES FUN OF MY SISTER AGAIN, I'LL SNAP YOU LIKE TWIGS!! YOU BUNCH OF SPOILED LITTLE BRATS!"

He reached down and picked up a stick lying in the grass, held it up, and cracked it in half, then turned and walked up the driveway. The stick was small enough even I could've broken it, but I don't think that mattered. Gabby's brother had made his point.

Gabby got on the bus and sat in the seat behind the driver. (I had a feeling this was going to be her new usual seat.) The bus driver radioed to the bus garage at school to tell them what happened.

I couldn't hear what she said because as she pulled away from the curb, King of the Jerks Jackson yelled, "Is that guy nuts or what?! He spends so much time in the trees, he's gone squirrelly."

And everyone on the bus laughed. Everyone except Gabby. And me.

THREE REASONS WHY SIXTH GRADE IS A LIVING NIGHTMARE

1. I NEVER see AlliCam anymore; and when I do, all I hear is pom-pom politics. Stuff like Alicia's mad at McKenzie because she said one of the moves Alicia suggested looked like something you'd see in an X-rated movie. Then Alicia said, "Whatever. Like <u>you've</u> even seen one." And then McKenzie threw a pom-pom at her.

Audra, the eighth-grade captain, isn't talking to Jackie Swanson because she says she's the biggest flirt at Crestdale Heights, and she says if Jackie even <u>thinks</u> of stealing her boyfriend, she'll make her life so miserable she'll wish she was never born.

And Ms. Jenson's mad at the whole squad because one day when they were supposed to run the track for a warm-up, all the girls sat behind the bleachers and talked. (The equipment boy for the football team told on them. Now they're planning to write fake secret admirer notes to him for revenge.)

The whole thing is worse than a soap opera, and since I don't have a starring role, all I want to do is scream at the top of my lungs, "WHO CARES?!!!"

2. I have nothing to do after school. I have nothing to do on the weekends. I have no one to call. I have no one to e-mail. I have no one to text message. I have no one to hang out with. Did I mention I have nothing to do?

3. I've come down with a strange sickness: "Gabby Guilt." Ever since I found out about Gabby's mom, I feel responsible for the misery of Gabby Marco. This is crazy because Gabby has been Crestdale Heights' biggest outcast since fourth grade. How could I possibly be responsible for that? I wasn't the one to call her "flabby." I wasn't the one to make fun of her house. I'm not the one who makes her laugh out loud for no reason at all. (She does that all by herself.)

So why do I feel like I've done something wrong? I can't change what everyone thinks. I can't make the other kids stop laughing. And I certainly can't stop Jackson Dawber from being his usual stupid self. (I'm pretty sure nobody can do that.) But even so, my Gabby Guilt is like a bad mosquito bite. I scratch it and scratch it, but the more I scratch it, the more it itches. And it just won't go away.

FIVE QUESTIONS MY MOM ASKS ME PRACTICALLY EVERY DAY WHILE I MOPE AROUND THE HOUSE

1. Why don't you give Alli and Cami a call?
2. Have you made any new friends in sixth grade you'd like to invite over?
3. Do you want to make some cookies with me?
4. Why don't you finish that scarf you're knitting?
5. Can't you find <u>something</u> to do?

FIVE ANSWERS I'D LIKE TO GIVE MY MOM BUT DON'T

1. Because I'm not a <u>real</u> pom-pom girl.

2. New friends, Mom? Really, do you remember at all what middle school was like?

3. C'mon, Mom, I'm not five.

4. Seriously, Mom, a scarf?

5. The only thing I WANT to be doing is the only thing I CAN'T be doing.

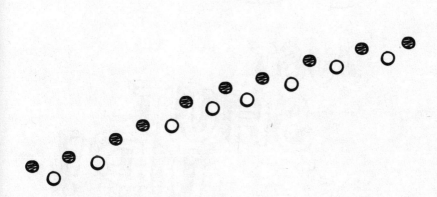

ONE QUESTION MY BROTHER ASKS ME EVERY DAY

What's YOUR problem?

THE ONE THING I'D LIKE TO SAY TO HIM BUT DON'T

JUST SHUT UP!

THREE REASONS WHY I DIDN'T SLEEP OVER AT CAMI'S HOUSE THIS WEEKEND

1. I would've been the only NON-pom there.

2. If I heard any more pom-pom politics, I was afraid I might barf all over everyone's sleeping bags.

3. Most of all, I knew that AlliCam didn't really care if I came or not.

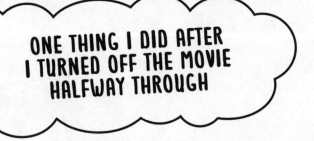

TWO THINGS I THOUGHT ABOUT WHILE I TRIED TO WATCH A MOVIE BY MYSELF FRIDAY NIGHT

1. No poms = No AlliCam

2. But what did no AlliCam = ?

ONE THING I DID AFTER I TURNED OFF THE MOVIE HALFWAY THROUGH

Finished reading *A Wrinkle in Time*, which I had borrowed from Old Hawk's classroom library.

THREE REASONS I STAYED AFTER SCHOOL MONDAY TO HELP OLD HAWK

1. Staying after school would earn me ten extra credit points, and I needed the points because I'd bombed my last vocabulary test.

   I wouldn't have cared so much, but I didn't want to get another note from Old Hawk listing all the things I was lacking. I was <u>supposed</u> to be living up to my mother's potential.

2. I needed to find ways to keep myself from devouring the rest of the 100-calorie snack bags left in our pantry.

3. I needed <u>something</u> to do. Anything. Willingly volunteering to help Old Hawk was proof of how desperate I was.

THE REASON I WISHED I HADN'T VOLUNTEERED TO HELP OLD HAWK

Gabby volunteered to help too.

THREE THINGS OLD HAWK SAID TO GABBY AND ME AFTER SCHOOL

1. "Remember, girls, you are earning extra credit points, so I expect a wholehearted effort."
2. "The storage cabinet is full of old books that have been there for years. It is in desperate need of being cleaned. Place the worn-out books in the trash. Save the ones that are in good condition."

3. "I will be attending a faculty meeting. Please mind your p's and q's while I'm gone and get down to brass tacks. I shall return in the hour."

SIX THINGS GABBY AND I DID AFTER OLD HAWK LEFT

1. Stared at each other for at least one full minute. (I kept waiting for Gabby to start laughing in her usual bizarro way, but she didn't.)

2. I emptied the top shelf of the storage cabinet onto the floor, and Gabby took an empty box from the back counter. We both sat down in the middle of the pile of books.

   "Too bad these are all picture books," Gabby said. "I collect old paperback books."

   What was Gabby? A librarian in training? I mean, I liked books, but c'mon, no normal person I knew "collected" old paperbacks.

3. We both picked up books from the heap and tossed them into the throw-away pile or put them into the save box.

   It was strange that Old Hawk's classroom library of novels was so elaborate and organized, when this pile of picture books was a mess.

4. After ten minutes, Gabby broke the silence with, "I LOVE this book!" She was holding a copy of *The Little Engine That Could*. It was tattered and worn, and pages were falling out. Gabby tossed it into the throw-away pile.

   I loved that book too. My mom had read it to me so many times that I knew the first page by heart.

   I wondered who had read the book to Gabby. Was it her mom? And did seeing the book remind Gabby of her? I wanted to say something, but what could I say?

5. Just after Gabby found *The Little Engine That Could*, I found another one of my favorite books, *Alexander and the Terrible, Horrible, No Good, Very Bad Day*. After this year I could write my own book. *Abigail and the Terrible, Horrible, No Good, Very Bad Year Of Sixth Grade*.

6. Gabby kept finding books she remembered and loved, and she made comments about each one. I kept finding books I remembered and loved, but I kept my mouth shut. I was helping Old Hawk for the extra credit points, not to become "book buddies" with Gabby Marco.

THE TERRIBLE, HORRIBLE, NO GOOD, VERY BAD THING THAT HAPPENED ON THE WAY TO CATCH THE LATE BUS

Since we had stayed after school to help Old Hawk, Gabby and I had to take the late bus home. All the kids on sports teams and pom-poms take it too. I didn't want the pom girls to see me getting on the bus with Gabby. I knew J&M would have something snotty to say about that. So I took my time getting my stuff out of my locker. I made sure Gabby left ahead of me. I must've stalled a little too long because I was still at my locker when I heard the driver toot the horn, signaling that the bus would leave in sixty seconds. I knew I was going to have to run. Running to the bus isn't such a horrible thing. I'd done it lots of times before. It's what happened <u>while</u> I was running to the bus that was the terrible, horrible, no good, very bad thing.

We'd had too much rain in the last few days, and whenever that happened, the parking lot on the side of the building always flooded. In order to get to the bus, everyone used the sidewalk alongside the water. That's where the terrible, horrible, no good, very bad thing happened. I slipped off the sidewalk and fell into the big parking-lot-sized puddle of water. I was sitting in the water looking up at a busload of pom-pom girls, basketball players, and volleyball players, wondering if I had just made myself the new outcast of Crestdale Heights. The laughter coming from the bus windows made me feel worse than the wet jeans I'd have to sit in on the way home.

Before I could even get up, Gabby headed out the doorway of the bus. She grabbed my backpack and helped me up.

She said, "Just remember, I think I can. I think I can. I think I can."

As I followed Gabby to the bus, water dripped from every seam of my jeans. When I looked up, I saw all the pom girls, faces plastered against the bus windows, staring at me and laughing. Even AlliCam.

All I could think was, "I can't come back to school tomorrow. I know I can't. I know I can't. I know I can't.

THE REASON I HARDLY SLEPT THAT NIGHT

I tossed. I turned. I sighed. I tried <u>everything</u> not to think about how AlliCam hadn't gotten off the bus to help me out of the puddle. I tried <u>everything</u> not to think about everyone laughing. I tried <u>everything</u> not to think about what J&M would be saying tomorrow about Gabby helping me.

When I finally fell asleep, I woke up a couple of hours later, and all I could think about was Gabby. She was the only person who <u>had</u> helped.

I wouldn't have helped her if she had fallen. I would've been one of the people at the bus window staring, and probably laughing too—not because I thought it was so funny, but because I wouldn't have wanted to be the only one <u>not</u> laughing. Knowing that about myself made me feel even worse than falling into the puddle.

145

TWO REASONS I FAKED SICK AND STAYED HOME FROM SCHOOL THE NEXT DAY

1. The terrible, horrible, no good, very bad puddle incident.

2. Gabby Guilt—it was giving me a headache. I didn't know why I was so worried about Gabby when I had plenty of my own problems. It's not as if me being nice to her would change her status at Crestdale Heights. Especially with the condition of <u>my</u> status. So what was I feeling so guilty about?

TWO THINGS MY MOM DID WHEN I STAYED HOME SICK

1. Made me my favorite rice pudding.
2. Let me use her laptop to watch a movie in bed.

TWO THINGS I DID THAT MADE ME FEEL WORSE

1. Acted grumpy.
2. Acted ungrateful.

TWO REASONS WHY I WISHED I WASN'T SO MEAN TO MY MOM

1. She was being really nice to me.
2. Gabby didn't even have a mom to be mean to.

ONE THING I WROTE THE NEXT MORNING ON THE MIRROR IN THE BATHROOM WHEN MY MOM WAS IN THE SHOWER

Thx, Mom!

U R the BEST!

A

TWO THINGS I FOUND IN MY FRIENDLY LETTER MAILBOX WHEN I WENT BACK TO SCHOOL

1. A piece of spiral notebook paper with all the assignments I'd missed written in Gabby's handwriting.
2. A note from Gabby. (Not a friendly letter. A note.)

Hey Abigail,

Old Hawk wants us to finish cleaning out the metal cabinet. She said she'd negotiate with us for more extra credit points. With all these extra points, LA will be an easy A, so I'm in. How about you?

Gabby

P.S. I can't stay after to do it today. How about tomorrow?

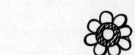

A NOTE I WROTE HOPING IT WOULD GET RID OF MY, NOW DAILY, GABBY GUILT HEADACHE

Gabby,

Okay. Tomorrow.

Abigail

THREE THINGS THAT HAPPENED THE NEXT DAY WHILE CLEANING OUT OLD HAWK'S CABINET

1. Gabby found *The Three Billy Goats Gruff* and said, "Oh, remember when that storyteller came to our class in first grade and told us this story?"

   I hadn't thought about it in a long time, but I did remember. How could I forget? The guy made the story so scary every first-grader had nightmares for a week.

   "WHO'S THAT TRIPPING OVER MY BRIDGE?!!!!" Gabby bellowed.

   She sounded so much like the storyteller guy, I got chills on the back of my neck.

   "It seems pretty stupid now, but I made my brother sleep in my room for a month after that child-abusing storyteller visited our classroom," Gabby confessed.

   "I slept with the lights on for the rest of the year," I said.

   Gabby seemed surprised that I agreed with her,

but she kept talking. "Yeah, for the longest time, I thought for sure there was a troll living under my bed."

2. After our troll phobia connection, we got back to work. That's when Gabby started her usual bizarro laughter, and for some reason it made the lava in my volcano start to heat up again.

At least this time I didn't try to tackle her. I just yelled, "WHAT? WHAT'S SO FUNNY? DON'T YOU KNOW EVERYONE THINKS YOU'RE CRAZY WHEN YOU LAUGH LIKE THAT?!!!"

Gabby didn't even look startled that I'd yelled, and she didn't even answer my question. All she said was, "Doesn't the troll look just like Jackson Dawber?"

"Are you crazy?" I asked, disgusted with myself for wasting any time feeling guilty about Gabby being an outcast when she was such a freak.

"No, seriously. Look at this picture. It looks just like Jackson," she said, pointing to the book. I looked at the book. Gabby was right. The troll's hair looked just like Jackson's moussed-up hairdo (which he thought made him look cool). The troll's chin was pointy and stuck out just like Jackson's. (His stuck out even more when he thought he was being funny.) And their noses were almost identical (which meant that Jackson Dawber had been born with a troll nose). That <u>was</u> something to laugh about.

I burst out laughing, and Gabby snorted like a pig, which only made us laugh harder. "I told you!" Gabby said, taking a breath. "They should make a copy of this picture and put it in the yearbook next to Jackson's photo."

I leaned back and laughed even harder and hit my head on the metal cabinet. Gabby snorted again.

Wiping tears away, I said, "Jackson Dawber, most likely to become a troll."

And that just made both of us collapse in hysterics on the piles of books lying on the floor.

They always say, "Laughter's the best medicine," and at that moment, I felt cured from all my Gabby Guilt.

3. We were still laughing by the time we heard Old Hawk clearing her throat as she walked back into the classroom.

"Are my friendly letter partners becoming too friendly?" she asked as she sat down at her desk to grade papers. "Remember why you are here, young ladies. I do not award extra credit points for horsing around."

We were quiet again until Gabby started making troll faces at me. I giggled to myself like Gabby usually did. The harder I giggled, the more faces Gabby made.

"Girls..." Old Hawk scolded, without looking up from her desk.

I felt like I would explode from laughter, but it was so much better than feeling like an active volcano.

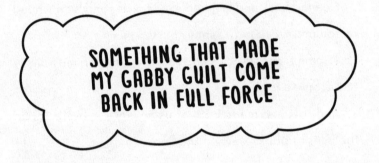

SOMETHING THAT MADE
MY GABBY GUILT COME
BACK IN FULL FORCE

Because of the terrible, horrible, no good, very bad puddle incident, I had asked my mom to pick me up so I wouldn't have to ride the late bus. But the puddle wasn't the only reason I'd asked her to pick me up. The other reason, the bigger one, was Gabby. I didn't want anyone on the late bus seeing us together and thinking we were friends.

I knew that made me a terrible, horrible, no good, very bad person. But I couldn't help it.

Already SPF with AlliCam was evaporating one letter at a time, and the other girls on the pom squad couldn't care less about me. If anyone thought I was actually friends with Gabby, that would be the final straw. I'd be another wannabe wandering the middle school halls without anyone even knowing I was alive, or worse, like Gabby, I'd become the punch line in Jackson's newest joke.

So when after leaving Old Hawk's room, Gabby said, "Let's stop at the water fountain before we head out to the bus. All that laughing made me thirsty."

I lied and said, "I have a dentist appointment, so my mom's picking me up." That's when the Gabby Guilt hit me like a bad flu, and I was sure I was going to throw up.

I walked to my mom's car feeling like a bigger troll than Jackson Dawber.

A NOTE I FOUND IN MY FRIENDLY LETTER MAILBOX THE NEXT DAY

Dear Abigail,

You and Gabby seem to have become fast friends. How simply delightful that an assignment meant to improve proper letter writing techniques has accomplished so much more.

Mrs. Carwell, our lead kindergarten teacher, requested that I recommend a couple of sixth-grade students to be guest readers for the classrooms in her wing. You and Gabby would be perfect for the job!

If all goes well, you would be given permission to skip homeroom once a week. In addition, it would enable you to earn points toward your middle school service requirement.

Please come to see me about it by the end of the week. I look forward to talking with you!

Sincerely,

Miss Hendrick

FIVE THINGS I THOUGHT AFTER READING THE NOTE

1. Missing homeroom once a week would be great!

2. I used to babysit for a couple of kindergarten-aged kids, and I loved them. They were so cute!

3. Gabby and I could practice the stories after school, and that would give me something to do.

4. Getting service points for reading to little kids was <u>way</u> better than visiting a smelly nursing home or picking up trash at the park.

5. THERE'S NO WAY I CAN DO IT!

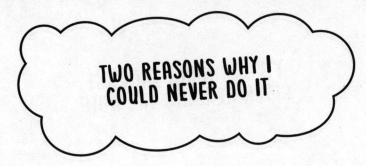

TWO REASONS WHY I COULD NEVER DO IT

1. I might as well tattoo the word "LOSER" on my forehead if I volunteered for this job with Gabby.

2. I could just hear J&M when they found out. "Abigail's hanging out with Gabby Marco? Maybe we need to find an alternate for our alternate."

THE NOTE GABBY LEFT IN MY LOCKER AFTER HOMEROOM

Dear Abigail,

Can you believe Old Hawk wants us to read to the kindergartners? We could be like the storyteller guy that came to first grade. (Only we wouldn't scare the kids half to death.) Pretty easy way to earn service points, huh?

Gabby

THE NOTE I STUFFED INTO GABBY'S FRIENDLY LETTER MAILBOX AFTER MATH

Gabby,

Reading to a bunch of bratty five-year-olds sounds lame. I've got better things to do. Forget it.

Abigail

THE THING I WROTE AT LEAST 100 TIMES ALL OVER THE INSIDE COVER OF MY SOCIAL STUDIES NOTEBOOK WHEN I SHOULD'VE BEEN TAKING NOTES

"I am A BIG FAT JERK!" I wrote it in my neatest, fanciest handwriting.

THE NOTE I FOUND IN MY FRIENDLY LETTER MAILBOX IN LA

Abigail,

That's cool. Little kids aren't for everyone. I should know. I babysit a lot. The extra money is great, but sometimes the kids are a real pain.

We got our extra credit points, relived the whole *Three Billy Goats Gruff* nightmare, and had a few troll laughs. What more can you want?

Later,
Gabby

THE ONE CORRECTION I MADE TO THE INSIDE COVER OF MY SOCIAL STUDIES NOTEBOOK WHILE I STARED OUT THE WINDOW AND WATCHED THE LITTLE KIDS PLAY ON THE PLAYGROUND

I am the BIG<u>GEST</u> FA<u>TTEST</u> JERK!!!!!!!! In the world!!!!! (Now it didn't look so neat and fancy, but it didn't look nearly as ugly and messy as I felt.)

THE REASON I WISH I COULD MELT INTO THE FLOOR LIKE THE WICKED WITCH OF THE WEST

In LA we played Spelling 500—Speedway for Super Spellers, a game only Old Hawk could dream up. I ended up on a team with Jackson Dawber, Brent Undervale, Melissa Stanson, and Gabby Marco.

As usual everyone on the team was ignoring Gabby. A couple weeks ago, that wouldn't have bothered me. But now it made my head throb. She'd covered for me when I tackled her. We'd sort of had fun helping Old Hawk with the books. And she'd helped me out of the puddle. I couldn't stop thinking about her mom being dead, and I didn't even want to know what the story was with her dad.

And what had I done? Totally blown her off. The least she could do was be mean to me. But she never was. It was enough to make a person gag.

We were on our final lap of Spelling 500. I needed to spell my word correctly to get our team over the finish line first. Lately my brain was so filled up with guilt, humiliation, and shame, I was having trouble concentrating. I was lucky to spell my name correctly. So of course, I missed the word, even though it was an easy one.

Jackson Dawber, troll boy that he is, said to Brent, "Falling in that puddle the other day must've knocked the sense right out of her."

Normally I would've been able to blow off something Jackson said, especially if he said it to someone like Brent, and especially if I deserved it for missing such an easy word. But because of the terrible, horrible, no good, very bad place I was in, my lava erupted.

I jumped up. I wanted to strangle the stupidity right out of him.

Gabby yelled, "Remember the troll!"

Her voice stopped me in midair, and I fell on the floor before I even touched Jackson. Gabby ran over and crouched down next to me and whispered, "Troll nose. Troll chin. Troll hair. It's all there."

The whole class gathered around Gabby and me like we were a car wreck on the side of the road.

"Miss Hendrick," Jackson said, pretending to be all

concerned, "I think our team needs some help from the pit crew."

Old Hawk rushed over when she saw us on the floor. "Good heavens! What is going on here, ladies?"

Gabby flashed me one of her lemons-into-lemonade business cards, and before I knew it, I was lying on the floor laughing in Gabby's bizarro way until I started to cry.

SEVEN THINGS OLD HAWK SAID TO ME WHEN SHE MADE ME STAY AFTER CLASS

1. "Abigail, what is the meaning of these inappropriate outbursts?"

2. "First, you tackle your dear friend Gabby Marco." (I knew Old Hawk hadn't believed Gabby's cover-up story.)

3. "Now you disrupt a perfectly lovely game of Spelling 500 by lunging at Jackson. Who, no doubt, somehow deserved this, but that is beside the point."

4. "You seem to be forgetting that in middle school it is important that you be striving to not only excel academically, which by the way you are struggling to do, but also to excel in the area of becoming a well-mannered young lady. Controlling your temper is of the <u>utmost</u> importance."

5. "And furthermore, your mother would be appalled at this kind of behavior."

6. "Now I suggest you begin using some type of anger management coping strategy, such as counting to ten,

or you will be counting your steps as you march your-

self straight down to Mr. Buckley's office."

7. "Are we clear, young lady?"

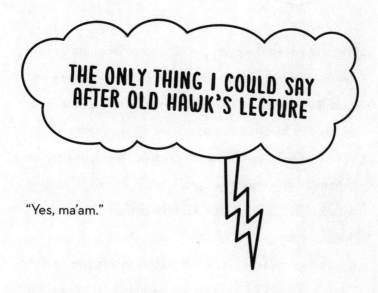

THE ONLY THING I COULD SAY
AFTER OLD HAWK'S LECTURE

"Yes, ma'am."

THREE THINGS THAT HAPPENED THAT DAY AT POM-POM PRACTICE

1. When I got to the gym, the girls were laughing behind my back about the terrible, horrible, no good, very bad puddle incident. As soon as they saw me, they pretended to be sympathetic.

2. Alli, fluttering her mascara-crusted eyelashes (since when did <u>she</u> wear mascara?), said, "You must've <u>died</u> when that 'flabby freak' Gabby got off the bus and helped you."

   She sounded exactly like Jackie when she said it. She even cracked her gum like Jackie.

3. I felt the lava inside me start to heat up. Silently I counted 1...2...3...and in my mind, I stirred the simmering lava.

THE REASON WHY IN MY HEAD I HAD TO COUNT WAY PAST TEN

I was mad at J&M and supermad at AlliCam for laughing at me. But deep down, I was even more furious with myself for not telling Alli to shut up when she called Gabby a flabby freak. But how could I?

THE REASON WHY OLD HAWK'S ANGER MANAGEMENT PLAN DIDN'T END UP MAKING ME VERY LADYLIKE AND WELL-MANNERED

As I counted well past one hundred, I kept picturing myself smothering each of the pom-pom girls with their own pom-poms. But Old Hawk's warning about being sent to Mr. B's office was fresh in my mind, so I held myself back. The lava continued to simmer inside me. Pretty soon, my head felt like it would explode.

THREE THINGS MY MOM ASKED ME WHEN I GOT HOME

1. What's wrong?
2. Are you sick?
3. Do you want to talk about anything?

THE THREE ANSWERS I GAVE

1. Everything.
2. I wish I <u>were</u> sick so I could stay home from school. Forever.
3. Did you ever wish you hadn't been so mean to someone?

ONE THING MY MOM SAID

Yes.

ONE THING I ASKED

What did you do about it?

ONE ANSWER MY MOM GAVE

Figured out how to make it right.

THE ONE THING ABOUT MY MOM'S ANSWER

I already knew what I had to do before my mom even answered my question.

TWO REASONS WHY, EVEN THOUGH IT WAS FAR, I WALKED TO GABBY'S HOUSE ON SUNDAY

1. I <u>had</u> to apologize to her, for everything.
2. Walking so far would be a good way to punish myself for being so mean.

THREE REASONS I WAS SCARED TO GO TO GABBY'S HOUSE

1. I was afraid of what it might look like inside the dented-up trailer barn house.
2. Her tree-climbing, crazy brother might be home.
3. I really didn't know what I was going to say.

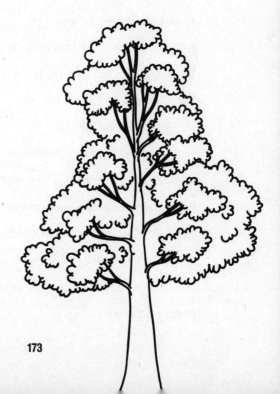

FOUR THINGS THAT HAPPENED WHEN I GOT TO GABBY'S

1. The knot in my stomach tightened when Gabby's lumberjack brother, Paul Bunyan, came to the door. He was dressed in a clean sweatshirt and jeans that looked new, not the tree-climbing flannel shirt and ripped pants he'd worn when he came to terrorize the kids on the bus. He smelled like an oak tree.

   When I said I was there to see Gabby, he smiled through the screen door of the dented-up trailer barn house.

   "You must be Abigail."

   I couldn't believe he knew my name. My older brother barely knew Cami's and Alli's names, and we'd been friends since we were five.

2. He said Gabby was babysitting somewhere in the neighborhood. He told me to wait so he could get some paper. He wanted to write down my name and phone number.

I didn't really want to leave my name and number with a crazy lumberjack, but because he seemed so happy that someone had come to see his sister, I just stood there on the porch, and he disappeared into another room in the house.

3. While he was gone getting the paper, I peeked through the screen door to see what it was like inside. Surprisingly, the house wasn't bad. The furniture and carpeting weren't new, but they were clean. The living room was picked up. No weird odors, except for the oak tree smell. The History Channel was on the TV in the corner showing *Ax Men: Man vs. Mountain*. I always wondered what kind of people watched that show.

In the corner on a card table, I noticed a stack of old paperback books, some boxes, and a few rolls of clear packing tape. I knew the books were probably part of Gabby's "collection," but what were the boxes and tape for?

4. Paul Bunyan came back, opened the screen door, and handed me the paper and pen. I scribbled my name and number on the memo pad and handed it back to him. "Gabby'll be sorry she missed you," he said. "Things have been kinda hard, well, since you know...I'll have her call you."

Paul let the screen door close, and I felt my Gabby Guilt headache turning into a migraine.

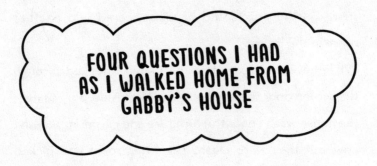

FOUR QUESTIONS I HAD AS I WALKED HOME FROM GABBY'S HOUSE

What did Paul Bunyan mean when he said, "Things have been kinda hard since..."?

1. Since what? Since her mom died?
2. Since kids started making fun of her?
3. Since she started laughing for no reason at all?
4. Since I started being a big fat jerk to her?

THE REASON I DIDN'T WRITE AN APOLOGY NOTE TO GABBY

Even if I used every one of Old Hawk's vocabulary words, there would <u>never</u> be enough of the right words to apologize for how I'd been treating Gabby.

THE REASON I DIDN'T SLEEP THAT NIGHT

Gabby never called.

FOUR THINGS THAT HAPPENED ON THE BUS THE NEXT DAY

1. I sat with AlliCam and stared out the window while they argued about whether Audra Marshall used fake tanning lotion or not.

2. Gabby got on and sat in her new usual seat behind the driver. She didn't even look at me.

3. Jackson Dawber tossed someone's shoe up the aisle of the bus. He was smart and threw it low enough so the driver didn't see. It hit Gabby in the calf. She turned around and gave Jackson a nasty look. (She knew he had done it because everyone was pointing at him.) She passed the shoe back.

   The whole thing would've been over if Jackson wasn't such a moron.

   "If your calves weren't as big as cows, it never would've hit you!" he yelled. Jackson's audience laughed. And when he started saying, "MOO! MOO!" AlliCam started giggling.

Since when did <u>they</u> think Jackson was funny? They both turned around, and Alli said, "Oh, Jackson, you're hysterical."

4. All the attention gave Jackson the incentive he needed to be even more of a moron, which I didn't think was possible. He started singing to the tune of "Bingo."

> *"There was a farmer who had a calf that turned*
> *into a cow,*
> *G-A-B-B-Y,*
> *G-A-B-B-Y,*
> *G-A-B-B-Y,*
> *And Gabby was her name oh."*

AlliCam actually started clapping along.

That's when I knew an apology would never be enough. I couldn't just <u>say</u> I was sorry. I had to do something to <u>show</u> I was sorry.

A NOTE I PASSED TO GABBY DURING HOMEROOM

Gabby,

I changed my mind about the kindergartners. Let's do it!

Abigail

WHAT I SAID TO OLD HAWK AFTER THE REST OF THE CLASS HAD LEFT HOMEROOM

"Miss Hendrick, Gabby and I would like to volunteer to be guest readers in the kindergarten class."

A NOTE GABBY PASSED ME IN THE HALLWAY BEFORE FIRST PERIOD

Abigail,

Glad you changed your mind about reading!

Sorry I didn't call last night.

Got home late from babysitting.

Gabby

TWO QUESTIONS I ASKED MYSELF

1. When was the last time I babysat?
2. Why had I stopped?

TWO ANSWERS I CAME UP WITH

1. It was hard to remember, but I think it was last spring just after AlliCam stopped babysitting.
2. What I do remember was hating to miss out on time with AlliCam when I was babysitting.

ANOTHER THING I WONDERED

Why did all that seem like such a long time ago when it was only just last spring?

183

THREE THINGS THAT HAPPENED THE NEXT WEEK WHILE GABBY AND I PRACTICED AFTER SCHOOL

1. We found out that besides *The Little Engine That Could*, we both loved a lot of the same books. *Where the Wild Things Are* was one of our favorites, but we were afraid it might give the kindergartners nightmares.

2. We decided to make the kids laugh instead of scream, so we chose *Green Eggs and Ham*. The problem was that, while we practiced, we spent most of our time laughing. Gabby had this way of making her eyes really round and then pushing her chin down to make a big frown, and at the same time making her neck seem really long. Wearing the paper hat that we made, she looked just like the guy who didn't want to eat the green eggs and ham. It was hysterical.

3. We decided to memorize the book so we could story tell it instead of read it. We knew the kids would like that better.

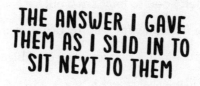

TWO QUESTIONS ALLICAM ASKED ME WHEN I GOT ON THE LATE BUS WITH GABBY

1. What are you doing with *her*?
2. You guys aren't *friends*, are you?

THE ANSWER I GAVE THEM AS I SLID IN TO SIT NEXT TO THEM

"You know I'm bombing LA with Old Hawk. I gotta get more extra credit points or my grade's going down the drain."

I didn't say it loud enough for Gabby to hear me.

The problem was, even though Gabby didn't hear me, I knew what I'd said, and the surge of guilt made my ears ring so loud they hurt.

THREE THINGS THAT HAPPENED THE NEXT WEEK DURING SCHOOL

1. Gabby kept trying to make me laugh during class by looking at me with the *Green-Eggs-and-Ham* face.

2. At first I held back the giggles, but finally I couldn't hold it in anymore. The hot lava inside me was turning into laughter. It felt good to let it seep out.

3. Jackson-the-Troll Dawber said to Brent in the hallway, "Gabby must've put a bizarro spell on Abigail because she's acting like a real reject lately."

   It made me wish I had some <u>real</u> green eggs and ham so that I could shove them down Jackson's throat, but I counted to ten instead.

SOMETHING GABBY AND I DID AT LUNCH

Came up with our own secret sign. When we walked by each other in the classroom or hallway, we held up our fist toward the other person and whispered, "That Gab-I-Am, that Gab-I-Am. I do not like that Gab-I-Am," Or, "That Ab-I-Am, that Ab-I-Am. I do not like that Ab-I-Am."

It wasn't a secret pom-pom girl wave, but it was still fun.

SOMETHING I WAS STARTING TO BE THANKFUL FOR

That AlliCam weren't in my homeroom.

A NOTE I GOT FROM GABBY

Abigail,

Can't practice today. I have to get to the post office after school and then babysit for the Welches. The kids are kind of a nightmare, but they pay really well, so I didn't want to say no. Need the extra money.

Sorry,
Gabby

P.S. Maybe we can practice before school.

ONE THING THAT SURPRISED ME ABOUT GABBY'S NOTE

It really bummed me out that we couldn't practice after school.

TWO THINGS I WONDERED AFTER READING GABBY'S NOTE

1. Gabby was ALWAYS babysitting. What did she spend her money on? Not clothes, that's for sure.

2. The post office? What did she have to go there for? I wondered if it had anything to do with the card table full of books, boxes, and packing tape I had seen in her living room.

TWO THINGS I WAS HAPPY ABOUT

1. That morning, Old Hawk put new books in each of our reading baskets.

2. She put *Island of the Blue Dolphins* in mine, so I added it to my list of things to take home so I'd have something to do after school.

FIVE THINGS THAT HAPPENED DURING OUR FIRST STORY TIME WITH THE KINDERGARTNERS

1. I was SOOOO nervous. I went to the bathroom six times before we started. Gabby was ready to kill me. She thought I was going to chicken out on her.

2. Mrs. Carwell, the kindergarten teacher, introduced us like we were somebody important.

   "Boys and girls, we are so lucky to have two wonderful guest readers with us today."

   The kids clapped like we were celebrities. To get them to stop clapping, Mrs. Carwell had to flick the lights on and off three times.

   Then she went on. "Let's be good listeners and keep our hands and feet to ourselves."

   It was amazing how she could smile the entire time she was talking as if her cheerfulness could will the kindergartners to behave.

3. When I announced the title of our story, one skinny kid in the back yelled, "I have that book!"

Then the girl sitting next to him said, "You do not!"

Then the boy punched her in the arm.

"Stanford, we do not hit. Especially girls," the teacher said, separating them.

I looked at Gabby, wondering if we'd made a big mistake volunteering to do this.

4. Finally, the teacher calmed everyone down again, and we started the story.

5. The kids gasped and laughed in all the right places. And when we said, "The end," they clapped and cheered and yelled, "Tell it again! Tell it again!"

FOUR THINGS THAT HAPPENED IN THE HALLWAY OUTSIDE THE KINDERGARTEN ROOM AFTER OUR FIRST STORY TIME

1. Gabby and I hugged each other and jumped up and down. I never knew it would be so much fun to tell a story to little kids. I shouldn't really have been surprised because it kind of reminded me how much I loved baby-sitting—I guess I hadn't realized how much I missed it.

2. As we hurried to our lockers so we wouldn't be late for first period, I heard someone call out, "Hey, Abigail!"

   It was AlliCam. They were standing by the drinking fountain outside the library.

   "You're not going to believe this!" they said, sprinting toward me. "Guess what we just found out in homeroom?"

3. When they got to where Gabby and I were standing, they each grabbed one of my arms.

   "Alicia Brenton broke her leg last night at gymnastics class," Cami said.

   "Jackie told us that her sister Janay, who's friends

with Alicia's sister, said that Alicia's probably out for the rest of the season," Alli continued in a rush.

"You know what that means?!" Cami asked.

"You're a pom-pom girl!" they both squealed, jumping up and down.

4. At first I only jumped along with them because they were still squeezing my arms. But as their excitement pumped through my body, the words sunk in: "You're a pom-pom girl!"

I was a pom-pom girl! For real. This was it! I wasn't an alternate anymore. My dream had come true!

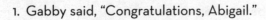

THREE THINGS THAT HAPPENED AFTER MRS. LANDERS, THE LIBRARIAN, STUCK HER HEAD OUT IN THE HALLWAY AND TOLD US ALL TO BE QUIET

1. Gabby said, "Congratulations, Abigail."

2. AlliCam rolled their eyes.

3. I cleared my throat and felt a Gabby Guilt migraine coming on.

EIGHT REASONS I COULDN'T FALL ASLEEP THAT NIGHT

1. I practiced each pom-pom routine in the bathroom in front of the mirror exactly six times, which is exactly half of the number of times that my mom yelled at me to turn down the music and get to bed.

   By the time I actually did get into bed, my heart was pounding faster than the beat of the music. I was wired.

2. So I got out of bed and tried on my pom-pom uniform <u>again</u>. I had picked it up from Ms. Jenson's office immediately after finding out about Alicia. I couldn't believe how great it felt standing in front of the mirror looking at myself in that uniform.

   But while I was admiring myself, I heard my mom coming upstairs to check on me, so I switched out the light, jumped into bed with my uniform on, and pulled up the covers. By the time she peeked in, I lay in bed with my eyes closed, breathing hard, since I had just done the ten-yard dash into bed. It looked like I'd been asleep for hours.

3. Once my mom left, I got up and practiced my smile in the dresser mirror. I wanted it to be perfect for the pom squad yearbook photo.

4. Finally, when my cheeks were tired from all that smiling, I took off my uniform and put on my pj's again. By this time, I was more wide awake than a rooster at five a.m.

5. That's when the headache that had started earlier that day in the hallway at school came back in full force. My head hurt so bad it felt like that five a.m. rooster was inside my brain trying to peck its way out.

6. Every time I closed my eyes, I saw myself jumping up and down in the hallway. Sometimes I was jumping up and down with Gabby. Sometimes I was jumping up and down with AlliCam.

7. One thing I was worried about. Now that I would officially be a pom, would J&M be nicer to me?

8. Every time I opened my eyes, I looked at my alarm clock. Each minute that blinked by was closer to seven a.m., when my alarm would go off. Each minute closer to seven a.m. made me feel further and further away from sleep.

THE NOTE I FOUND ON THE KITCHEN COUNTER THE NEXT MORNING

Hey Abs,

Congrats about poms!

There's a celebration doughnut in your lunch.

Love,

Dad

TEN THINGS ALLICAM AND I TALKED ABOUT ON THE BUS

1. How exciting it was that I was finally a real pom-pom girl!

2. Ditto

3. Ditto

4. Ditto

5. Ditto

6. Ditto

7. Ditto

8. Ditto

9. Ditto

10. Ditto

THE ANNOUNCEMENT THAT CAME OVER THE LOUDSPEAKER BEFORE HOMEROOM BEGAN

"Ms. Jenson's out sick, so pom squad practice is canceled for today."

My DESTINY would be delayed one more day.

THE THANK-YOU NOTE FROM MRS. CARWELL, WHICH OLD HAWK READ OUT LOUD IN HOMEROOM

Dear Gabby and Abigail,

Thank you so much for coming to our class. The children have not stopped talking about you. One of them asked me if you two are Dr. Seuss's kids.

ONE THING JACKSON DAWBER WHISPERED TO BRENT WHILE OLD HAWK WAS READING THE LETTER
(OF COURSE HIS WHISPER WAS LOUD ENOUGH FOR A FEW KIDS NEARBY TO HEAR, BUT NOT QUITE LOUD ENOUGH FOR OLD HAWK TO HEAR.)

"Dr. Seuss maybe. Dr. Stupid for sure."

If I hadn't been so tired, I would have punched him, but I barely had the strength to get mad about it.

ONE THING OLD HAWK ASKED BEFORE CONTINUING TO READ THE LETTER

"Is there something you would like to share with the rest of the class, Mr. Dawber?"

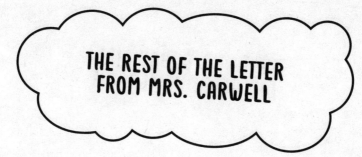

THE REST OF THE LETTER
FROM MRS. CARWELL

The boys and girls drew pictures to thank you for spending time with us. We do hope you will come back soon.

Love,
Mrs. Carwell's Kindergarten Class

THE THING GABBY AND I DID AFTER HOMEROOM

We looked at all the pictures the kindergartners had made for us. Some were of me in my Sam I Am hat, holding up the plate of green eggs and ham. Some were of Gabby in her hat, scrunching up her face, getting ready to eat the green eggs and ham. And some were pictures that didn't have anything to do with *Green Eggs and Ham*. But they were all cute! And they were for us!

THE THING THAT HAPPENED WHILE WE WERE LOOKING AT THE PICTURES FROM THE KINDERGARTNERS

Other kids leaving homeroom tried to look over our shoulders to see what the pictures looked like. And I knew no matter what Jackson Dawber or anyone else said, they were wishing the pictures were for them. I could just feel it. It was the same feeling I'd had when I thought I'd made captain of the pom squad.

SOMETHING I SAID TO GABBY WHILE WAITING FOR ALGEBRA TO START

"I want to show these pictures to my mom and dad."

TWO THINGS I THOUGHT ABOUT AFTER I SAID IT

1. Gabby didn't have a mom to show them to.

2. Did she have a dad?

SOMETHING GABBY SAID AFTER THAT

"Yeah, I think I'll ask Old Hawk to make copies so I can send them to <u>my</u> dad."

> ## THE ONE QUESTION I WANTED TO ASK GABBY, BUT DIDN'T

Where <u>is</u> your dad anyway?

> ## THE REASON I DIDN'T ASK GABBY ABOUT HER DAD

Whatever the answer was, I was worried that it would somehow make me feel even more guilty.

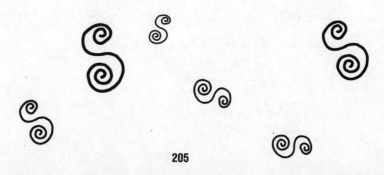

THINGS TO DO

1. Ask Old Hawk if I could take a few of her picture books home.

2. Read the picture books tonight and find another good one for Gabby and me to read to the kindergartners.

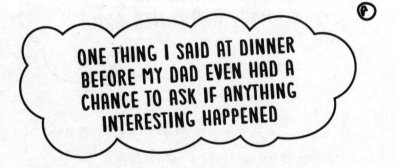

ONE THING I SAID AT DINNER BEFORE MY DAD EVEN HAD A CHANCE TO ASK IF ANYTHING INTERESTING HAPPENED

"Wait 'til I show you the cute thank-you notes the kindergarten kids gave Gabby and me."

TWO THINGS MY BROTHER SAID

1. "Are you talking about Gabby Marco?"

2. "Didn't her brother drop out of school to become a lumberjack or something?"

THE THING I SAID THAT SORT OF SURPRISED ME
(ACTUALLY THE <u>WAY</u> I SAID IT IS WHAT SURPRISED ME)

"He's a tree climber, and it's superdangerous. And for your information, he <u>had</u> to quit school to take care of Gabby."

> ## THE ONLY THING MY NEANDERTHAL BROTHER SAID BEFORE STUFFING AN ENTIRE DINNER ROLL INTO HIS MOUTH

"Cool."

> ## THE LIST OF BOOKS I SHOWED GABBY THE NEXT DAY THAT WE COULD MAYBE USE FOR OUR NEXT STORYTELLING WITH THE KINDERGARTNERS

1. *Sylvester and the Magic Pebble*
2. *Stone Soup*
3. *Miss Nelson Is Missing!*
4. *Abiyoyo*
5. *Jack and the Beanstalk*

THREE THINGS I'LL ALWAYS REMEMBER ABOUT MY FIRST PRACTICE AS A <u>REAL</u> POM-POM GIRL

1. The minute I walked into the gym, AlliCam and J&M saluted me with the secret wave. Then they ran to me screaming, surrounding me with their pom-poms, and I knew right then that I was NOT an alternate anymore. And when Jackie put my very own "POMS FOREVER" T-shirt over my head, I felt like I'd just been crowned Miss America.

2. Jackie liked my idea for the ending pose of our second routine, and since she was the squad's captain, she said we'd probably use it at our next game.

3. The whole basketball team walked through our practice on the way outside to run laps. I swear Kip Thompson winked at me. I almost passed out.

   All my pom-pom dreams were coming true.

THE NOTE I FOUND ON THE FLOOR
THE NEXT DAY IN THE HALLWAY
OUTSIDE ALLICAM'S LOCKER WHEN I
STOPPED BY TO LEAVE THEM A NOTE

AlliCam,

What's with Abigail and Gabby? They aren't friends, are they?
Doesn't she know she's part of the Fab Five now?

Poms Forever,
J&M

THE ONE THING I WANTED
TO DO BUT <u>DIDN'T</u> DO AFTER
READING THE NOTE

Cry.

THE ONE THING I <u>DID</u> DO AFTER READING THE NOTE

Crumpled up the note that I'd planned to leave in AlliCam's locker and threw it away.

It said:

AlliCam,

Poms for real is even better than I dreamed, and J&M are soooo great!

SPF,
Abigail

211

THE THING THAT HAPPENED THE NEXT AFTERNOON AT PRACTICE

The fire alarm went off. Ms. Jenson filed us out into the parking lot. The fire department showed up. Right away they said it wasn't anything serious. A small fire in the faculty bathroom, which made sense, since we saw smoke coming out of the window. They said we wouldn't be getting back into the building anytime soon. Ms. Jenson decided to have us practice out in the field, but when she realized Jackie and Alli couldn't stop drooling over the cute firemen, she decided to cancel practice. I was glad. I couldn't concentrate anyway.

All I could think about was Gabby. <u>Were</u> we friends?

All I could think about was the Fab Five. Were <u>we</u> friends?

All I could think about was poms. Was this the way it was supposed to be?

WHAT WE FOUND OUT THE NEXT DAY ABOUT THE FIRE

A stink bomb had started the fire. Mr. Buckley found out it was Jackson who lit it. It was his own dumb fault he got caught because he left an extra stink bomb in his locker. It was out in plain view when Old Hawk had us do our weekly locker cleanup. Now Jackson's in HUGE trouble. Besides an in-school suspension, Mr. Buckley is making Jackson earn twice as many service points by the end of the school year. Looks like Jackson will be putting down his highlighter-microphone and picking up a broom, a shovel, and a trash bag full of litter. Worse than that. If he doesn't watch it, come summertime, he'll be packing his bags for bad-boy boot camp just like his brother did last summer.

> # FIVE THINGS THAT HAPPENED IN THE NEXT FEW DAYS THAT MADE IT SO GREAT TO BE PART OF THE FAB FIVE

1. I got to do the "secret wave" in the hallway with all the other poms, even the seventh- and eighth-graders.

2. I was finally part of the inside jokes and pom-pom politics with AlliCam.

3. Maddie Jacobson, a seventh-grade pom, told me she loved my gym bag, and now she has one just like it.

4. Kip Thompson said hi to me in the hall exactly three times <u>and</u> smiled at me in the cafeteria.

5. We have a game on Friday, and I get to wear my uniform to school. I CAN'T WAIT!!!

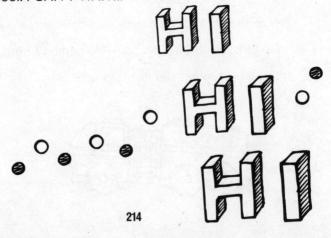

THE NOTE FROM MS. JENSON THAT REMINDED ME EVEN MORE JUST HOW GREAT IT WAS TO BE A POM

Dear Sixth-Grade Pom Squad,

Yearbook photos will be taken two weeks from Saturday. We will meet in the main gym that morning at 11. Be prompt and be sure both you and your uniform are at their best.

Ms. Jenson

ONE REASON MS. JENSON DIDN'T NEED TO REMIND US TO BE PROMPT AND PREPARED FOR THE POM SQUAD YEARBOOK PHOTO

Being in the pom squad yearbook photo was one of the BEST parts about being a pom. None of us would ever be late.

ONE AWESOME THING ALLICAM SAID WHEN WE GOT THE NOTE ABOUT THE YEARBOOK PHOTO

"Abigail's the Queen of Lists! Let's have her write a to do list for our pom squad photo shoot."

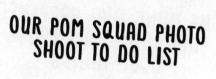

OUR POM SQUAD PHOTO
SHOOT TO DO LIST

1. The day before the photo shoot, meet at Jackie's house for manicures.

2. The morning <u>of</u> the photo shoot, meet at McKenzie's at 6 a.m. to get ready.

3. Take turns doing each other's hair.

4. Take turns doing each other's makeup.

5. Put on uniforms.

6. Head over to school by 10:30.

ONE THING THAT HAPPENED THAT RUINED ALL THOSE GOOD THINGS

Gabby and I had switched our practice time to before school so I could go to poms after school. But on Thursday, Gabby couldn't come before school, so we had to do a quick run-through of our latest story for the kindergartners before I went to poms.

I had thought about telling Gabby to forget the whole reading thing, but I knew if I did that, my Gabby Guilt might turn into a permanent pain in the neck that might just last the rest of my life. Besides, I could only imagine the speech I'd get from Old Hawk if I backed out now. I decided it was just easier to stick with it, but that was before Jackie brought it up in front of the whole squad.

When I got to practice, Jackie asked Ms. Jenson in front of everyone, "Won't it be a conflict for Abigail to be on poms <u>and</u> be a little storyteller for the kindergartners?"

Thankfully, Ms. Jenson basically told her to mind her own business. She really said, "I'm sure Abigail and I can work that out."

But as soon as Ms. Jenson went to check on the seventh- and eighth-grade squads, Alli whispered to McKenzie, "Gab-Agail, Gab-Agail, tell me your tale."

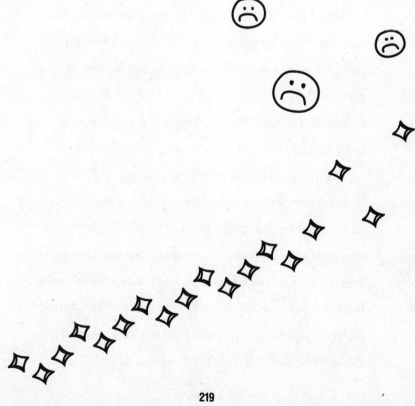

ONE THING THAT MADE THE CAFETERIA'S TUNA CASSEROLE TASTE LIKE THE BEST LUNCH I'D EVER EATEN

It was Friday, game day, and I was feeling great in my pom uniform. I didn't think it was possible, but I was about to feel even better.

After I paid for my lunch, I headed toward my usual spot next to Jeannie and Marcy. This is when my life changed in an instant. I looked up to see Kip waving me over to sit by him.

At first, I thought he must be waving at someone else, but when he smiled that cute, dimpled smile, there was no mistaking it. He was smiling at me.

I was so nervous, I don't know how I even walked all the way to his table without dropping my tray or tripping or something. I sat down across the table from him, acting as casual as I could, but it wasn't easy because inside my head I was screaming, "I'M EATING LUNCH WITH KIP THOMPSON!!! HOW CAN THIS BE HAPPENING??!! WAIT 'TIL I TELL ALLICAM!!"

Kip didn't talk much. I talked even less. I'd been so busy being geeked about Kip liking me, I'd never even thought about what I might say to him if I actually had the chance to talk to him.

But it was still the best school lunch I'd ever tasted.

THE NOTE I WROTE TO ALLICAM RIGHT AFTER LUNCH

Dear AlliCam,

Question of the day:

Which pom-pom girl just ate tuna casserole in the cafeteria with the Kip Thompson?

You get one guess.

Give up?

ME!! ME!! ME!!

Can you believe it?!!!!!!!!!!!!!!

SPF,

Abigail

A NOTE I FOUND IN MY
FRIENDLY LETTER MAILBOX

Hey Abigail,

How about me tagging along with you and Flabby when you read?
I NEED SERVICE POINTS!!! BAD!!!

Jackson

WHAT I SAID TO GABBY AFTER I SHOWED HER JACKSON'S NOTE

"NO WAY!!!!!"

ONE THING GABBY SAID AFTER I SAID, "NO WAY!"

"Think of all the great troll stories we could do."

THE THING I SAID AFTER THAT

"Jackson's such a troll he'd scare the kids worse than the child-abusing storyteller that came in first grade. Besides, after all that mean stuff he's done to you? Forget it."

But as soon as I said it, my stomach tightened up like a ball of aluminum foil. I mean, I was being a little nicer to Gabby now, but I felt like deep down there was an ugly troll inside me too. I didn't make fun of Gabby out loud like Jackson did. But I still didn't want anyone thinking we were friends. And I knew I would never be able to stand up for Gabby if it meant putting my reputation on the line. Did that make me an even <u>bigger</u> troll than Jackson Dawber?

WHAT I FOUND IN MY LOCKER AFTER SCHOOL THAT MADE ME FORGET ALL ABOUT TROLLS

ABIGAIL + KIP = TRUE LOVE FOREVER (TLF) with hearts all around it written on the cover of every single one of my spiral notebooks and folders.

AlliCam must've gotten my note.

THREE GOOD THINGS THAT HAPPENED AT MY FIRST GAME AS A REAL POM-POM GIRL

1. Even though I was nervous (I thought for sure I would pee my pants), I did the whole routine perfectly.

2. We used my pose idea at the end of the song, and the crowd went crazy.

3. Kip was looking at ME the entire time we were out there.

THREE BAD THINGS THAT HAPPENED AT MY FIRST GAME AS A REAL POM-POM GIRL

1. Gabby showed up and sat in the front row of the bleachers.

2. She kept smiling at me the whole time and giving me the thumbs-up sign.

3. I'm pretty sure I saw Kip looking at Gabby and giving her the "how-can-you-be-here-when-you're-such-a-loser" look.

TWO THINGS THAT HAPPENED AFTER THE GAME

1. Jackie said, "My mom's waiting in the parking lot to drive us all to Chitchat. Let's go!"

    We all grabbed our gym bags and poms and headed toward the door. Going to Chitchat in my uniform was like the cherry on top of a hot fudge sundae.

2. Gabby stood at the edge of the bleachers. I know she saw me, and I think she could tell that I saw her. I pretended not to notice her, and it felt like the ice cream on my sundae was melting and the cherry was sliding off, so I hurried out the door before it fell all the way to the floor.

THREE THINGS THAT HAPPENED AT CHITCHAT THAT MADE ME FORGET ALL ABOUT GABBY

1. We sat in the corner booth, and <u>this</u> time I wasn't sitting on a chair. I had a great spot right next to Jackie.

2. Jackie said, "I propose a toast to Abigail on her first game. Move over, Alicia Brenton, because Abigail Walters is in the house."

   Everyone cheered, raised their soft drinks, and tapped their straws together.

3. When the boys came over, Kip slid into the booth <u>right</u> next to me. He smelled so good I thought I would faint.

ONE THING I DIDN'T NEED

The list of interesting things to talk about with the seventh- and eighth-grade poms because this time I was definitely part of the group.

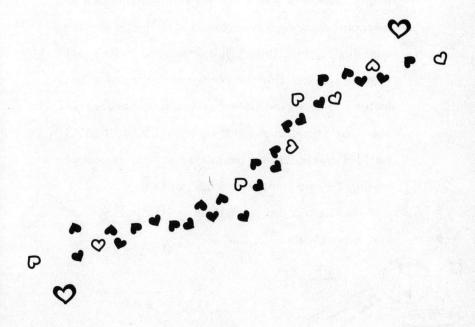

ONE THING THAT HAPPENED LATER THAT NIGHT

I lay in bed thinking about what kind of house Kip and I might live in if we got married. But when I fell asleep, I dreamed about Gabby.

In the dream, she was sitting in the gym on the empty bleachers. I was in the middle of the basketball court shooting free throws, and all the poms were cheering for me. Then Gabby came down to shoot free throws too. But the poms didn't cheer for her. Instead, they waved their pom-poms in her face so she couldn't see. Just as I tried to say, "Stop it! That's not fair!" the buzzer for the game clock blared. It kept blaring. No one could hear what I was saying.

I woke up, with my alarm blasting. I felt sweaty, tired, and out of breath.

THINGS TO DO SATURDAY

1. Look up Gabby's phone number online.
2. Call her.
3. See if she wants to get together and practice the story we're working on.

FIVE THINGS THAT HAPPENED LATER THAT DAY

1. Gabby's brother dropped her off at our house.

2. We made costumes for our next story, "The Gingerbread Man."

3. We practiced our lines and made up actions to go along with the story. Gabby even made up new words for the song in the story to make it more fun for the kids.

   Instead of always saying, "Run, run as fast as you can..." Gabby thought it would be fun to say different things every time, like, "Wiggle, wiggle as fast as you can..." or "Dance, dance as fast as you can..." and then let the kids do what the song said. We knew the kindergartners would love to wiggle and dance.

   Gabby always had such great ideas!

4. When we got hungry, I asked my mom if we could make gingerbread cookies. She said no, because we didn't have the stuff, but she said we could make chocolate chip cookies instead.

5. We spent the rest of the afternoon making cookies, and even though they weren't gingerbread cookies, we decorated them anyway.

ONE THING THAT HAPPENED WHILE WE MADE COOKIES

Gabby called her brother to ask if she could stay a little longer. She ended up staying for dinner. Mom let us make frozen pizzas and eat while we watched TV.

ONE THING I REALIZED WHILE WE WATCHED TV

All my Gabby Guilt had vanished.

THE QUESTION I ASKED LATER WHILE
WE SAT IN THE DARK LIVING ROOM
WAITING FOR GABBY'S BROTHER
TO COME AND PICK HER UP

"Where *is* your dad anyway?"

GABBY'S ANSWER

"In jail."

WHAT I SAID NEXT

Nothing.

I was completely speechless.

WHAT GABBY FINALLY SAID TO FILL THE SILENCE

"When my mom got sick, my dad started drinking, and when she died, he drank even more. He got arrested for leaving me home alone. It's called neglect. The judge is making him serve two years in jail because he was arrested for it so many times."

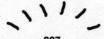

THREE THINGS THAT HAPPENED NEXT

1. A horn honked outside.
2. Gabby thanked me for inviting her over.
3. She gave me a quick hug and ran out the door.

WHAT HAPPENED AFTER THAT

I sat in the dark living room thinking about what Gabby had told me. Before I knew it, my head was buried in my hands and I was crying.

ALL THE THINGS I WAS CRYING ABOUT

1. Gabby's mom dying.

2. Gabby's dad being in jail.

3. Gabby always getting teased and made fun of.

4. Gabby not having any friends.

THE ONE THING THAT MADE ME SOB THE HARDEST

Gabby needed a friend more than anyone at Crestdale Heights, and I was probably the only person who knew that. But I still didn't want anybody to know we were friends.

THE ONE THING THAT MADE ME SOB EVEN HARDER THAN THAT

Gabby was always nice to me, no matter what.

THE NOTE I LEFT NEXT TO THE COFFEEPOT BEFORE I WENT TO BED

Dear Dad,

Thanks for all the doughnuts.

Love,
Abs

SOMETHING ALLICAM ASKED ME ON THE BUS ON MONDAY

"Gabby Marco was over at your house ALL DAY Saturday?!!!"

THREE THINGS I DID INSTEAD OF ANSWER THE QUESTION

1. Swallowed hard.
2. Started to sweat.
3. Felt my head throb. It wasn't Gabby Guilt this time.

   It was "AlliCam Anxiety."

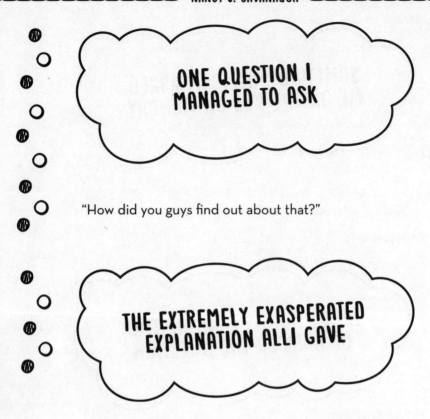

ONE QUESTION I MANAGED TO ASK

"How did you guys find out about that?"

THE EXTREMELY EXASPERATED EXPLANATION ALLI GAVE

"My mom heard it from your mom at their book club last night. She said you guys were singing songs and making cookies. What's going on, Abigail? You told us you were only hanging around with her to get extra credit points for Old Hawk.

"You get extra credit points for making cookies at your house on Saturday? I don't think so. I mean really, Abigail, we're the Fab Five. You gotta remember that.

242

Plus, did you forget that one of the cutest, most popular guys in the whole school likes you? You know how lucky you are? <u>Every</u> girl wants Kip to like her. You better not blow it by hanging around with <u>Gabby</u>."

ONE THING I THOUGHT ABOUT AS I WALKED TO HOMEROOM

A seesaw.

My life was a seesaw. AlliCam on one end. Gabby on the other. I was in the middle trying to keep both sides from crashing to the ground.

It was impossible!

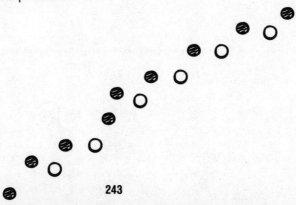

243

THE NOTE I FOUND IN MY FRIENDLY LETTER MAILBOX

Hey Abigail,

Sat. was a blast! The kids are going to <u>love</u> "The Gingerbread Man," especially our new version of the song.

    I got this idea that we could make gingerbread cookies to give to all the kids after the story. So I had my brother take me to the store to get the stuff so we could make some.

    What day do you want to get together to do it?

    Would your mom let us make them at your house?

Let me know.

Gabby

WHAT I THOUGHT ABOUT DURING FIRST PERIOD

I wanted to come clean with everyone about my friendship with Gabby, especially because of what she told me about her parents, but also because she really was my friend. Saturday at my house had been a lot of fun.

But if I let people know we were friends, the Fab Five would flip out. It could mean the end of all the pom fun and popularity. I couldn't risk that.

SO THIS IS THE NOTE I
WROTE BACK TO GABBY
ABOUT MAKING COOKIES

Gabby,

I have pom practice every day.
I'll have to let you know.

Abigail

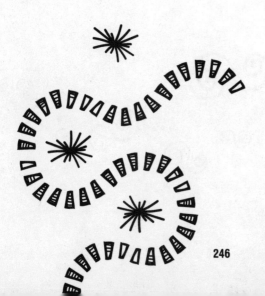

246

THREE GREAT THINGS ABOUT LUNCH THAT DAY

1. It was pizza. My favorite.

2. Kip had saved me a spot at his table.

3. Gabby wasn't in the cafeteria because she had signed up to volunteer in the office once a week. Today was her day. I was relieved. I had managed to avoid her all morning, and now that she wasn't in the cafeteria, I could relax and enjoy my lunch with Kip.

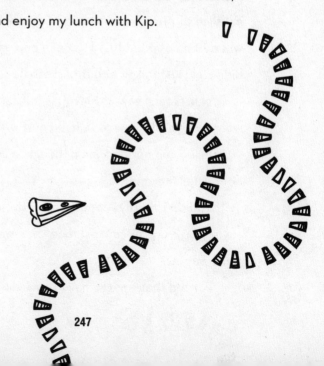

247

THE REASON WHY I COULDN'T RELAX AND ENJOY MY LUNCH WITH KIP

I was waaaaaay toooooooo NERVOUS!

The first time I'd eaten with him, it had been a surprise, so I hadn't had time to think about it. But now my mind was racing with all the ways I might completely embarrass myself.

So I let him talk while I took really small bites of my slice of pizza. I was worried he'd ask me a question when I had a mouthful of cheese and sausage. But he didn't. He just talked about basketball.

"Yeah, Coach says my layup is our fast break secret weapon against Elmwood's half-court press."

I smiled and nodded, even though I had no idea what he was talking about.

I couldn't really concentrate on what he was saying anyway because I had too many things to think about.

I worried that I might have pizza sauce on my face

or a piece of oregano in my teeth. Then I was paranoid that everyone in the cafeteria was staring at us.

Were they wondering why such a cool guy like Kip was sitting with someone like me? Thinking about that made me wonder the same thing.

 But then Kip said something so sweet:

"The poms are so much better now that you're on the squad."

All my nervousness melted, and I felt as warm and cozy as hot chocolate and marshmallows.

SOMETHING EVEN BETTER THAT HAPPENED WHEN THE LUNCH BELL RANG

After Kip carried my tray to the trash, he offered me a piece of spearmint gum. I knew what that meant. AlliCam and I had read it in one of our magazines last summer. "When a boy offers you gum or mints, it's usually a sign that he wants to kiss you."

THE NOTE I SCRIBBLED
TO ALLICAM THE FIRST
CHANCE I HAD

AC,

Kip gave me gum!!!!

SPF,

A

THE NOTE ALLICAM SCRIBBLED BACK THE FIRST CHANCE THEY HAD

A,

GUM!!!! OMG!!!!

SPF,

AC

WHAT I DID THE REST OF THE AFTERNOON IN ALL MY CLASSES

I drew more hearts and TLFs all over my folders and spiral notebooks.

251

THREE REASONS WHY THE SEESAW I WAS ON WAS BEGINNING TO FEEL MORE LIKE A ROLLER COASTER

1. Gabby kept bugging me about making cookies, and I kept making excuses.

2. AlliCam kept making sure the three of us were together ALL THE time, so I couldn't spend any time with Gabby.

3. I kept making sure I was everywhere Kip was and kept wondering if he really did want to kiss me. Thinking about that made me excited and petrified all at the same time, which ended up making me feel like I might throw up any minute.

FOUR REASONS WHY MY ROLLER COASTER WAS PICKING UP SPEED

1. I never made cookies with Gabby, but she showed up to our story time with a boxful of supercute gingerbread cookies. One for each of the kids. They loved them! She even made extra cookies for the teacher. She said her brother helped her make them.

   I felt like a slug.

2. McKenzie heard from a girl on her bus that Gabby and I had done "The Gingerbread Man" story, so at practice on Thursday, she and Jackie kept singing, "Run, run as fast as you can. Flabby can't catch you, but Abigail can."

   Of course, they only did it when Ms. Jenson wasn't around.

3. Gabby showed up to the basketball game on Friday night and sat in the front row, AGAIN.

4. Kip kept giving her weird looks AGAIN.

THE WONDERFUL, YET HORRIBLE THING THAT MADE ME REALIZE I HAD TO GET OFF THE ROLLER COASTER

The poms went to Chitchat after the game. We had a great time—talking, laughing, joking. It was so fun I felt like I was in a movie. It was just the best! And then it got even better when the basketball players showed up.

Kip actually made someone move so he could sit right next to me. I told him he played great. He told me I <u>looked</u> great! Then he talked about each point he made in the game. After that, he talked about how many times he stole the ball from the other team. It was like listening to my favorite song on the radio over and over. I could've listened to him talk all night.

And finally, when most of the other kids had moved to different tables, Kip offered me another piece of gum. I couldn't believe it! I was going to get my first kiss right there in Chitchat. How awesome was that?

I felt the excitement of speeding down the biggest hill on a roller coaster.

Scary but FUN!

Kip leaned a little closer to me, but then things took a sharp turn, the way roller coasters sometimes do, jerking you in a completely different direction.

He said, "You gotta lose Flab Girl."

"What?" I asked, confused that my exhilarating ride had just turned into something that could give a person whiplash.

"Gabby," he said. "You really got to lose her. She's a freak."

I didn't know what to say, but I didn't have time to say anything because someone yelled, "C'mon, Kip! Brandon's dad's here to take us home."

"See ya, Abigail!" Kip said, and he got up and was gone.

WHAT I DID THAT NIGHT WHEN I GOT HOME

Wrote two lists.

THINGS ABOUT KIP

1. Cute ☺
2. Cool ☺
3. Great smile ☺
4. Athletic ☺
5. Likes me ☺
6. I <u>think</u> he wants to kiss me. ☺

THINGS ABOUT GABBY

1. Always have fun together ☺
2. Always covers for me ☺
3. Bizarro laughter ☹
4. Crestdale Heights biggest outcast ☹

WHAT I DID AFTER MAKING THE LISTS

Wrote two math equations:

1. 2 ☺ s + 2 ☹ s = A Big Fat Zero
2. But are 6 ☺ s <, >, OR = A Big Fat Zero?

Both equations were easy, but solving the problem was impossible.

I knew if I blew off Gabby it would mean I was a worse troll than Jackson Dawber. But at the same time, it would mean Kip would be happy, which meant I'd probably be getting that kiss soon. I could go on as part of the Fab Five living the blissful, popular life of a pom-pom girl, and no one but Gabby would know I was a troll.

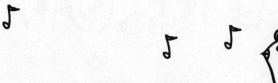

THE NOTE I GAVE GABBY ON MONDAY

Gabby,

You can probably tell how demanding it is being a pom-pom girl. I really have to focus on this opportunity. After all, I'm representing our school. Anyway, I'm not going to be able to do the story thing with you anymore. I'm sure you understand.

Abigail

THE LETTER I GAVE OLD HAWK

Dear Miss Hendrick,

I know you are going to be disappointed in me, but I am quitting the kindergarten storytelling. You probably know I am a pom-pom girl now. This takes a lot of my time, and I feel I cannot devote the appropriate effort to reading to the younger children.

Sincerely,
Abigail Walters

GABBY'S REPLY

Okay.

Good luck,

Gabby

OLD HAWK'S REPLY

Dear Abigail,

You more than disappoint me, you surprise and shock me. To commit to something and then decide not to fulfill that commitment is simply unacceptable. I was counting on you. Mrs. Carwell was counting on you. And those darling little kindergartners were counting on you too. That's not to mention your dear, new friend Gabby Marco.

I can only hope that you do not make this a pattern in your life. If you do, my friend, you will find yourself going down a very dangerous and treacherous path.

Sincerely, your very disappointed teacher,
Miss Hendrick

P.S. And I have not forgotten that temper of yours. I'm keeping my eye on you.

THREE WONDERFUL THINGS THAT HAPPENED IN THE NEXT WEEK

1. With Gabby and Old Hawk off my back, I felt great. (Old Hawk's lecture had been hard to take, but I found that when I crumpled up her letter and threw it in the cafeteria Dumpster, I felt A LOT better about it. I mean, I wasn't trying for the teacher's pet award, so why should I care if Old Hawk liked me or not? In fact, her whole sinister warning about my life going down a "dangerous and treacherous" path was actually sort of funny.)

2. I got an invitation to McKenzie's birthday party. The party was in two weeks. It was at the bowling alley, and her parents were letting her invite boys. The only kids invited were pom-pom girls and basketball players. It would be the perfect crowd! More importantly, it would be the perfect place for my first kiss.

3. After practice, Kip always sat with me on the late bus. Having his sweaty leg touching mine was the best, most

wonderful, terrifically awesome thing that has ever happened to me in my entire life.

ONE THING THAT MADE ME REALIZE I WASN'T REALLY OFF THE ROLLER COASTER

Complete and utter exhaustion. Every night in that magic moment just before I drifted off to sleep, something in my brain made me think of Gabby.

I thought about how much fun it had been reading to the kindergartners. I thought about all the notes and pictures the kids gave us. I thought about how much fun Gabby and I had practicing after school, and all the fun we'd had that day at my house. And then I thought about what it must be like to be Gabby—having a mom who was dead and a dad who was in jail.

The problem was that Gabby wasn't the only one who knew how much of a jerk I was. I knew too. I knew *every* minute, of *every* day, and it was making it impossible to enjoy *anything*.

Every night, no matter how tired I was, or how close I was to falling asleep, I'd always think about Gabby, and I would instantly be wide awake. It was like that moment when you put a quarter in the lights at the park tennis courts. One minute pitch black. The next minute bright as daylight. And the night would drag on and on. Most nights I don't think I even slept at all.

THE OTHER THING THAT MADE ME REALIZE I WASN'T REALLY OFF THE ROLLER COASTER

I found one of Gabby's paperback books on the floor in the hallway outside our homeroom. It was a copy of *Julie of the Wolves*. On the inside cover in Gabby's handwriting, it said,

Dear Dad,

Can't wait to hear what you think. I loved this book! It reminds me of *Hatchet*.

The jokes and drawings you sent me in *Shiloh* were hysterical. I don't know how you think up such funny stuff.

Love you,
Gabby

P.S. Pete says hi.

I flipped to the back cover and there was a message from her dad.

My Gabriella,

Loved it! You know how to pick 'em. You're so strong! I'm so proud of you!
So happy you like my cartoons!

Love,
Dad

P.S. Your mom has to be smiling all the time when she sees what you've become.

Gabby and her dad wrote to each other in the margins of old paperback books? This was Gabby's paperback collection?

I flipped through the book and noticed the margins were full of little cartoon drawings with captions underneath them. Some were related to the story and some were random, but almost all of them were really good and superfunny.

THE POSTER ALLICAM AND
I SAW IN THE HALLWAY
BEFORE HOMEROOM

FROG & TOAD PRODUCTIONS
—— PRESENTS ——

THE THREE BILLY GOATS GRUFF

DIRECTED BY

STORYTELLING TEAM
GABBY MARCO & JACKSON DAWBER

CHARACTERS PLAYED BY:

BILLY GOATS: VOLUNTEERS FROM THE AUDIENCE

TROLL: JACKSON DAWBER

NARRATOR: GABBY MARCO

ONE THING I THOUGHT ABOUT WHEN I SAW THE POSTER

Gabby and I had talked about making posters for our stories, but we had never gotten around to it. I had sort of been looking forward to writing the titles of the stories in fun, fancy letters with big, fat colored markers. I could've made the poster look so cool, but this one didn't look that great because neither Gabby or Jackson had very nice handwriting. But the way the poster looked wasn't really the problem. It was the way the poster made me feel that I was having a hard time with.

THREE THINGS THAT HAPPENED NEXT

1. Alli said, "Jackson Dawber?! She teamed up with him?!
   She really _is_ a loser!"

2. When Gabby came around the corner, Alli joked, saying,
   "Frog and Toad Productions? Who's the frog and who's
   the toad?"

   "Does it really matter?" Cami continued. "If the wart
   fits, wear it!"

   AlliCam laughed, and I laughed right along with
   them, but my heart pounded so hard and my ears rang
   louder than the laughter. I tried not to look at Gabby,
   but even so, I saw her press her lips together and take a
   deep breath, and I wondered if she was thinking about
   her mom's saying about making lemonade.

3. Then J&M walked up, and Jackie looked at the poster
   and then at Gabby and said, "Gabby, really, you should
   just let Jackson crawl back into his hole. And you should
   do the same."

And the Fab Five high-fived each other. Then AlliCam and J&M did the secret pom wave to me and rushed off to homeroom.

THE ONE THING I DID NEXT

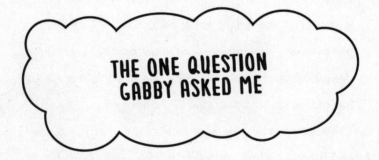

Nothing.

Gabby and I stared at each other.

I stood as still as a statue, wishing I could turn into stone so I would not be able to feel anything.

THE ONE QUESTION GABBY ASKED ME

"Do you have anything to say?"

MY ANSWER TO GABBY

I shrugged my shoulders and looked at the floor.

Even if I could've found my voice, what could I say?

TEN THINGS I THOUGHT AS GABBY STOOD STARING AT ME

1. NO ONE was a bigger jerk than I was.

2. Ditto

3. Ditto

4. Ditto

5. Ditto

6. Ditto

7. Ditto

8. Ditto

9. Ditto

10. Ditto

EVEN THOUGH I COULDN'T TALK, GABBY HAD PLENTY TO SAY

"I have something to say.

"You want to know why I'm working with Jackson Dawber? Because I had a <u>so-called</u> friend who dropped me like a hot potato. Yeah, the minute she had something better to do, she ignored me and avoided me all day, every day. Then, as if that wasn't bad enough, when she decided to notice me again, she laughed right along with her friends when they made fun of me. You're such a follower, Abigail! And do you know what? <u>You're</u> the real loser! Jackson Dawber might've made fun of me and teased me, but I can take that. At least he never <u>pretended</u> to be my friend."

ONE THING THAT HAPPENED RIGHT AFTER THAT

I turned around to go into homeroom and ran right into Old Hawk. I could tell by the look on her face that she had heard everything.

SINCE OLD HAWK HEARD EVERYTHING, I KNEW SHE WAS GOING TO PULL ME ASIDE AND TALK TO ME, BUT SHE DID SOMETHING MUCH, MUCH WORSE

Nothing.

I waited all day for her to talk to me, but all she ever did was look at me with that Old Hawk look. The one that said I had done something so terrible, so horrible, so no good, so very bad that even she, who always had something to say, didn't have anything to say at all.

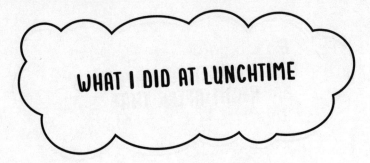

WHAT I DID AT LUNCHTIME

Instead of going to the cafeteria, I went into the bathroom, made sure no one was in there, and bawled my eyes out. I was the most terrible, horrible, no good, very bad person in the entire world.

I wished I could be someone else.

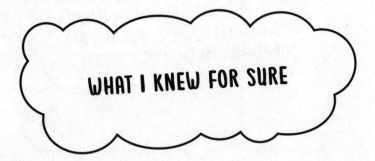

WHAT I KNEW FOR SURE

Everything Gabby said about me was true. She was right. *I* was the real loser. *I* was the one who should crawl into a hole.

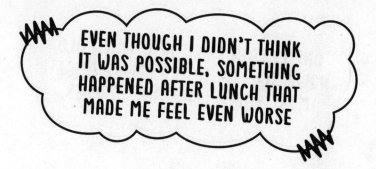

EVEN THOUGH I DIDN'T THINK IT WAS POSSIBLE, SOMETHING HAPPENED AFTER LUNCH THAT MADE ME FEEL EVEN WORSE

When I got back to class, Gabby came in late. I could tell she'd been crying. Gabby Marco, the girl who got teased and humiliated all the time and never cried, had been crying, and it was because of me.

I REALLY <u>was</u> the most terrible, most horrible, most no good, most very bad person in the entire universe.

ONE PERSON I RAN INTO WHEN OLD HAWK SENT ME TO THE OFFICE TO GET MORE PAPER CLIPS AND STAPLES

As I came down the hall, I saw Gabby's brother, Paul Bunyan, standing outside the office. Oh my gosh! Had he come to yell at me about how mean I was being to Gabby? Maybe he was going to wait outside in the parking lot until I came out after school. But just before I started to hyperventilate, I realized one of his arms was in a sling. And when he turned around to face me, I saw a huge bandage on his forehead, along with a lot of scratches and scrapes on his arms and face.

When he saw me, he said, "Hey, Abigail!"

"Hi," I said, not knowing whether to call him Pete or Paul.

"Man, on a day like today," he said, "I'm glad Gabby's got a friend like you."

Obviously he didn't know what had been going on between Gabby and me lately.

"What happened to you?" I asked.

"Fell out of a tree this morning," he answered.

"What?!"

"Yeah, I was up about ten feet at least. Still don't know what went wrong. Really don't know how that tree branch didn't land right on top of me, but the important thing is I'm all right."

"What are you doing here?" I asked.

"Came by to see Gabby. My boss called the school to let her know what happened. She's such a worrier. I knew she'd need to see me with her own eyes to believe I was okay. Can't really blame her for that. I'm all she's got. Has she stopped crying yet?"

My head was spinning so fast I felt like I was falling out of a tree. A very tall tree.

"She's doing a little better," I lied.

I figured a little white lie making someone who'd almost just died feel better was a good thing compared to the horrible, despicable things I'd said and done to Gabby.

277

ONE MORE THING THAT MADE ME FEEL EVEN WORSE

On my way to pom practice, I saw Jackson talking to Gabby in the hallway, and it looked like Jackson was actually being nice. I couldn't believe it! On a day when so many bad things had happened, Jackson had found a way to make Gabby smile. I was a big fat jerk, and Jackson was being nice?

What was going on here? My life wasn't a roller-coaster ride that was out of control; it was one of those crazy fun house mirrors. You know, the ones that make you look too short and too fat or too tall and too skinny, and you're supposed to laugh at yourself. The only problem was that there was nothing fun about the crazy mirror I was looking into right now. When I saw what I really looked like, there was nothing to laugh about.

THREE THINGS I BEGAN TO NOTICE ABOUT JACKSON

1. He didn't carry around his highlighter-microphone anymore.
2. He high-fived the kindergartners when he got on the bus, and they high-fived him back.
3. He and Gabby practiced together EVERY DAY after school.

THREE THINGS I BEGAN TO NOTICE ABOUT MYSELF

1. I was finally part of the pom-pom politics, but I wasn't sure I wanted to be.
2. Kip really liked me, but I wasn't sure I wanted him to.
3. I was part of the Fab Five, but I wasn't sure that was so fabulous.

THE FRIENDLY LETTER I FOUND IN THE RECYCLE BIN WHEN I WENT TO GET A PIECE OF SCRATCH PAPER

Dear Brent,

Well, it's military school for my brother, man. He was caught shoplifting last week and my dad went gonzo. He and Max got into this huge fight. I thought they were gonna kill each other. I went with my dad over the weekend to drop him off at the place. You should have seen it! It looks worse than a prison. It makes that bad boy boot camp he went to last summer look like a country club. Max was pleading with my dad not to leave him there, but we drove away anyway. It was harsh, man.

My dad didn't talk the whole way home until we got to our driveway. Then he turned to me and said, "You better not even THINK about getting into any more trouble because you'll be sharing a room with your brother so fast your head will spin."

Talk to you,

Jackson

TWO THINGS I THOUGHT ABOUT AFTER READING THE LETTER

1. Maybe Jackson really was going to change for the better.

2. Maybe I had already changed for the worse—on top of what I'd already done to Gabby, I had just committed a federal offense by reading Jackson's letter.

ONE THING I DID

Crumpled up the letter and shoved the evidence into my backpack.

ONE THING THAT HAPPENED THE NEXT DAY THAT MADE ME REALIZE FOR SURE THAT THE FAB FIVE WAS NOT SO FABULOUS

When AlliCam and J&M were talking by my open locker, Gabby's paperback book, the one I had found in the hallway, fell from the top shelf. It landed on the floor. I had wanted to give it back to Gabby, but the two of us weren't really speaking to each other, so I had just kept it in my locker.

Before I could pick it up, Alli grabbed it and asked, "What's this?"

Of course Jackie snatched it away from her before I could even answer. She opened it up and started reading.

"'Dear Dad, Can't wait to hear what you think...' What is this?"

"Just give it to me," I said.

Jackie turned to the back. "'My Gabriella...' Gabriella? Is this Flabby's? She writes love notes to her dad in books? She's even weirder than we all thought."

The four of them laughed and then, thankfully, the warning bell rang. Jackie tossed the paperback up in the air, and it fell to the floor. The cover bent back, and I hoped it didn't rip. Just then Gabby walked by. I reached down and tossed the book into my locker before she noticed it. Jackie had to be a jerk and say, "Hi, Gabriella!" in a real snotty way before she and McKenzie and AlliCam rushed off to class. I stood there feeling my face get hot as Gabby walked by me, gave me a sorry look, and went into homeroom.

ONE THING I KNEW FOR SURE ABOUT MYSELF

I <u>hated</u> who I was turning out to be.

ANOTHER THING I KNEW FOR SURE

I was miserable, every minute, of every day.

AND THE LAST THING I KNEW FOR SURE

I didn't know what to do about it.

THE REAL TRUTH

Actually I did know what to do about it.

I had to stand up for Gabby. And I had to stand up for myself.

THE EVEN MORE REAL TRUTH

I knew I could NEVER do that.

COWARD

THE TRAGIC PART OF THE TRUTH

If I ever did stand up for myself, poms, popularity, Kip, and probably AlliCam would all be history.

ONE THING THAT HAPPENED ON THE WAY TO LUNCH THAT MADE ME FEEL LIKE CRYING

I saw Jackson talking to Gabby at her locker, and he was making her laugh.

ONE THING THAT HAPPENED AFTER LUNCH THAT SHOULD HAVE MADE ME WANT TO EXPLODE WITH HAPPINESS

Kip left me a note in my locker:

Hey Abigail,

Are you going to McKenzie's party?

Do you want to go with me?

My dad said he'd drive us and pick us up.

See ya around,

Kip

THE ONLY TWO THINGS I COULD THINK ABOUT DURING MY AFTERNOON CLASSES

1. My first middle school party, and Kip wanted to take me.
2. I should've been the happiest girl in middle school.

THE ONE QUESTION I ASKED MYSELF
(EVEN THOUGH DEEP DOWN I KNEW THE ANSWER)

Why wasn't I?

THE BIGGER QUESTION
I ASKED MYSELF

Was I brave enough to do something about what I knew

deep down?

THE MOST TERRIBLE, HORRIBLE,
NO GOOD, VERY BAD THING THAT
HAPPENED IN THE HALLWAY LATER
THAT DAY AFTER SCHOOL

When I came down the hall on my way to pom practice,

I was thinking about telling Ms. Jensen I didn't feel well.

The last place I wanted to be was at pom practice, and

saying I was sick wouldn't really even be a lie. I <u>was</u> sick.

Sick of everything and everyone—poms, the Fab Five,

Kip, and most of all myself. I just wanted to go home, or

better yet crawl under a big rock and not come out for a very, very long time. Maybe never.

I saw a crowd of people outside the gym. When I got closer, I saw Kip.

I realized right away what was going on when I heard someone say, "Troll Prince Jackson probably kissed her, and that's how she got so ugly."

Gabby was kneeling on the floor on the other side of the hallway painting something on a piece of poster board. She acted like she didn't hear what everyone was saying about her, but she slid herself, the poster, and all her paints farther down the hallway away from the crowd and kept working on her sign. She had that weird bizarro-laugh look on her face.

Then I recognized Kip's voice saying, "Yeah, first she was an ugly toad. Then he kissed her, and she got even uglier."

Kip's cute, dimpled smile didn't look so cute anymore. I thought about his note in my pocket.

Jackie shook her pom-poms. "Give me a *U*!"

"*U*!" everyone shouted.

"Give me a *G*!"

"*G*!"

"Give me an *L*!"

"*L!*"

"Give me a *Y!*"

"*Y!*"

With each letter the crowd yelled, I felt the hot lava of anger and shame bubble closer and closer to the surface.

And when Jackie shook her pom-poms and yelled, "What does it spell?!"

I exploded like a volcano that had been brewing and boiling and bubbling for centuries.

"SHUT UP!!!" I screamed, running toward the group.

I threw my backpack and gym bag down. I rushed toward everyone, kicking and pushing backpacks and books that were in my path.

"SHUT!!! UP!!! JUST SHUT UP!!!"

My words were like hot, molten lava spewing everywhere.

"ALL OF YOU JUST! SHUT! UP!!!"

Everyone stood, frozen, staring at me.

I stopped screaming.

Breathing hard, I looked around at all of them.

No one knew what to do.

Notebook paper, folders, pens, and pencils that had spilled out of the open backpacks were scattered everywhere like the aftermath of a hurricane. It was like the calm after the storm.

Kids started giving each other weird looks.

I heard someone say, "That was random."

"Totally," someone else agreed.

A bunch of the seventh- and eighth-grade poms said, "Whatever," as they gathered up their bags.

Finally Mr. Harmon, the basketball coach, stuck his head out the gym door and blew his whistle. The basketball players grabbed their stuff and hustled into the gym, probably faster than they ever had before.

I turned around and picked up my stuff. I still didn't look at Gabby. I couldn't, but I could feel her looking at me from down the hall as I followed AlliCam and J&M into the sixth-grade practice room.

SHUT UP!

293

FOUR THINGS THAT HAPPENED BEFORE MS. JENSON GOT TO POM PRACTICE

1. Jackie said, "We better be careful what we say around here or Abigail might freak out." The four of them laughed.

2. "Maybe she should stick to reading picture books with her little frog and toad friends," Jackie said to McKenzie.

   "Just shut up," I said.

3. "You know," Jackie continued in her smarmy, sarcastic voice, "since you and Gabby get along so well, maybe your family could adopt her. Then you'd be sisters. Maybe she wouldn't be such a freak if her crazy brother wasn't raising her."

   "Jackie, you better shut your mouth!" My voice got louder.

   "Oooooh," Jackie said, pretending to be afraid. "What are you going to do? Tackle me or something?"

4. Jackie turned and whispered to McKenzie, loud enough for everyone to hear, "Can you believe she

really thought that the star by her name on the pom roster meant she was going to be captain?"

"The only thing she could be captain of is the kindergartners," McKenzie added.

"Or the freaks," Jackie said. "We should've hidden Ms. Jenson's note even longer."

I couldn't believe it! They'd hidden Ms. Jenson's note and let me think I'd been made captain of the squad? I wondered if AlliCam had known about that. How could I have even wanted to be part of this group?

Nobody said anything while the "malicious" (to use one of Old Hawk's vocab words) truth hung in the air.

Jackie and McKenzie threw their heads back and ran their fingers through their long, shiny, shampoo-commercial hair, as if they were waiting to be crowned Queen of Mean or something. AlliCam just stood there.

The silence felt full. Full of questions.

Would my best friends and so-called sisters stand up for me? Would I ever really be part of the Fab Five? Would I become the next Flabby Gabby of Crestdale Heights?

No one had the chance to answer any of those questions.

THE REALLY SURPRISING THING I DID

I laughed. I laughed like I'd never laughed before. In the most bizarro way I knew how.

THE REALLY SURPRISING THING THAT HAPPENED AFTER THAT

AlliCam and J&M didn't know what to do. And none of them had anything to say.

THE REALLY SURPRISING THING I REALIZED WHILE I WAS LAUGHING

Bizarro laughter was the ultimate secret weapon. It was the best way to turn lemons into lemonade.

It was not only how Gabby survived being the outcast, it was how she survived everything that happened to her. Her laughter took the power away from everyone and everything.

Gabby wasn't an outcast. She really was a genius.

TWO THINGS I DID AFTER I STOPPED LAUGHING

1. Felt Kip's note about McKenzie's party that was in my front jeans pocket.

2. Looked over at the bulletin board in the corner and saw the reminder Ms. Jenson had posted about the pom squad photos coming up in just two days. My to do list was posted right underneath it.

THE NEW TO DO LIST I THOUGHT OF IN MY HEAD WHILE EVERYONE CONTINUED TO STARE AT ME

1. Stand up for Gabby. ✓
2. Stand up for myself.

THE THING I SAID TO MS. JENSON WHEN SHE GOT TO PRACTICE

"I quit."

And AlliCam and J&M gasped like someone in the circus had just fallen from the high wire. And I put a check mark behind "Stand up for myself" on that to do list in my head.

THE THING I DID AFTER THAT

I went and sat on the late bus and waited for practice to be over.

THE THING THAT HAPPENED WHEN ALLICAM GOT ON THE BUS

They walked past my seat and sat in the back of the bus.

THE THING THAT HAPPENED WHEN KIP GOT ON THE BUS

He walked past my seat and sat across from AlliCam.

THE THING THAT HAPPENED WHEN GABBY GOT ON THE BUS

She saved a seat for Jackson.

THE THING MY MOM ASKED ME WHEN I GOT HOME

"Need me to wash your pom uniform for Saturday's pictures?"

THE ONE ANSWER I GAVE

"Yes, I need it washed, but not for pictures. I'm giving it back to Ms. Jenson tomorrow."

THE ONE THING THAT SURPRISED ME

My mom wasn't all that surprised when I told her what

happened.

THE PLACE I ASKED MY MOM TO DRIVE ME TO THAT NIGHT AFTER SUPPER

The bookstore.

THE THING I PUT IN GABBY'S FRIENDLY LETTER MAILBOX THE NEXT DAY

A copy of *The Little Engine That Could.*

THE THING I WROTE ON THE INSIDE COVER OF THE BOOK

Dear Gabby,

You're like the little blue engine—always willing to rescue someone who needs help. You make people do things they never thought they could do. Anyone who has you as a friend is lucky.

Even though there's no way to tell you I'm sorry, I want you to know that I am. And even though there's no reason for you to forgive me, I hope that maybe someday, maybe somehow, you will.

Your friend (I hope),

Always,
Abigail

THE BOOK I TOOK FROM OLD HAWK'S CLASSROOM LIBRARY THAT AFTERNOON DURING SILENT READING TIME

Hatchet.

I decided since Gabby liked it so much I should give it another try. Besides, it would be another book Gabby and I could talk about if she ever decided to forgive me.

> THE NEXT DAY I FOUND THE BEST THING EVER IN MY FRIENDLY LETTER MAILBOX

A copy of *The Three Billy Goats Gruff.*

WHY *THE THREE BILLY GOATS GRUFF* WAS THE BEST THING I'D EVER FOUND IN MY FRIENDLY LETTER MAILBOX

It was from Gabby.

305

THE THING GABBY WROTE ON THE INSIDE COVER OF THE BOOK

Dear Abigail,

I forgive you.

Hope you'll trip trap back to kindergarten and tell some stories with Jackson and me. (He's not as much of a troll as we thought.)

Your friend,
Gabby

(Next to her writing, Gabby had labeled the three billy goats on the title page—Jackson, Abigail, and Gabby. Underneath that she'd written, "We're a trio, so trolls don't scare us!")

TEN THINGS I LEARNED IN SIXTH GRADE

1. Pom-poms wasn't the best thing about sixth grade.

   (It ended up being the WORST thing.)

2. Being Gabby's friendly letter partner wasn't the worst thing about sixth grade.

   (It ended up being the BEST thing.)

3. Gabby and I love to talk even more than AlliCam and me. We've already had four sleepovers, and we haven't gotten one bit of sleep at any of them because we always stay up all night talking.

4. Gabby's dad will be getting out of jail in less than two months. He's finished a whole book of cartoons, and Gabby and I are going to turn some of them into stories to tell the kindergartners. Imagine how surprised he'll be.

5. Having Old Hawk for homeroom and language arts wasn't the worst part of sixth grade either.

   (It ended up being the other best part.)

6. Sister rituals don't really work. (Thank goodness.) AlliCam and I don't really talk much anymore, which is fine by me. Sometimes you just have to move on.

7. Kip Thompson might be one of the <u>cutest</u> guys in school, but he isn't the <u>coolest</u>. (He only thinks he is.)

8. When Jackson Dawber doesn't carry around his highlighter-microphone, he's not that bad of a guy.

    (The kindergartners actually love him.)

9. Laughter isn't just the best medicine; it's the best way to turn lemons into lemonade.

    (Which happens to be the cure for pretty much everything.)

10. A lot of things in sixth grade didn't turn out the way I planned. They turned out even better.

THE FRIENDLY LETTER I WROTE TO OLD HAWK AT THE END OF THE SCHOOL YEAR

Dear Miss Hendrick,

I have to admit, when I got to sixth grade, I wasn't too happy to be in your homeroom—for lots of reasons. But now, it's the end of the year, and I can honestly say, you're one of my favorite teachers—for lots of reasons.

Your friendly letter assignment, which I HATED in the beginning of the year, "literally" (aren't you proud I'm using one of your vocab words?) changed my DESTINY, so thank you!

Always,
Abigail

ALWAYS, ABIGAIL
DISCUSSION QUESTIONS

1. Do the characters in *Always, Abigail* remind you of people you know? If yes, who and why?

2. In what ways does Abigail change from the beginning of the book to the end?

3. Why is Gabby Marco so unaffected by the teasing and bullying?

4. Why does Jackson Dawber bully people? Why does he stop? Why do the pom girls tease and bully? Do you think they'll stop?

5. In what ways are Abigail and AlliCam alike? In what ways are they different?

6. Which character in the book would you like to be friends with?

7. How does Abigail feel about Old Hawk at the beginning of the book? How does she feel at the end? Why do her feelings change?

8. Do you think Abigail and Gabby would have become

friends without the friendly letter assignment? At what point in the story do you think they really become friends?

9. Why does it take Abigail such a long time to do the right thing? Do you think that happens in real life?

10. Do the events in *Always, Abigail* remind you of things that have happened in your own life or at your own school?

For more discussion questions, classroom activities, and a Common Core-aligned educator guide, visit www.sourcebooks.com/resources/educators-guide.html.

ACKNOWLEDGMENTS

In true Abigail fashion, eight important thank-yous:

1. To Dominique Raccah for building a company like Sourcebooks where an author like me gets to watch her stories become beautiful books.

2. To all my wonderful friends at Sourcebooks for all you do to make my books become more than I ever thought they could be. I'm so happy to be doing books with all of you!

3. To Aubrey Poole, my editor, for loving Abigail the same way she loved Ratchet and for knowing exactly how to help me make my characters and their stories the best that they can be. I absolutely LOVE working with you!

4. To Holly Root, my agent, for giving Abigail and me a chance. If it weren't for your belief in me and your persistence with my work, Abigail would still be a bunch of lists and letters tucked away in the bottom of a drawer. Thank you, thank you, thank you for being in my corner with me!

5. To my writing friends who make me a better writer and a better friend.

6. To my family who always supports me and now tells everyone who will listen that I am a published author.

7. To Ron and Chaylee for all the pom-poms of love and support you always wave for me. I couldn't do any of this without you, and I wouldn't even want to.

8. To God for blessings beyond what I could ask or imagine! My heart overflows with gratefulness.

ABOUT THE AUTHOR

Nancy J. Cavanaugh lives in Florida with her husband and daughter. She spends summers eating pizza in her former hometown of Chicago. *Always, Abigail* is her second middle grade novel. Her debut, *This Journal Belongs to Ratchet*, received the Gold Medal in the Florida State Book Awards and earned a *Kirkus* starred review.

Like Abigail, Nancy enjoys writing lists. Her secret to turning an unproductive day into a productive one is writing a few things on her to do list that she has already accomplished just so that she can cross them out.

In the past, Nancy's lists helped her stay organized as an elementary and middle school teacher and also a library media specialist. Presently, her lists help her organize her life as a writer. Nancy enjoys doing school visits and writing workshops as well as sharing teaching ideas with librarians and teachers at conferences. Visit her at www.nancyjcavanaugh.com for more information.